PENGUIN BOOKS

RUMPOLE AND THE REIGN OF TERROR

John Mortimer is the author of one Rumpole novel and twelve Rumpole collections, many of which formed the basis for the PBS-TV series *Rumpole of the Bailey*. His work also includes many award-winning novels and plays and three acclaimed volumes of autobiography. A former barrister at the Old Bailey, London's central criminal court, Mortimer, who was knighted in 1998, lives in Oxfordshire, England.

Rumpole and the Reign of Terror

JOHN MORTIMER

PENGUIN BOOKS

PENGUIN BOOKS
Published by the Penguin Group
Penguin Group (USA) Inc., 375 Hudson Street, New York, New York 10014, U.S.A.
Penguin Group (Canada), 90 Eglinton Avenue East, Suite 700, Toronto,
Ontario, Canada M4P 2Y3 (a division of Pearson Penguin Canada Inc.)
Penguin Books Ltd, 80 Strand, London WC2R 0RL, England
Penguin Ireland, 25 St Stephen's Green, Dublin 2, Ireland
(a division of Penguin Books Ltd)
Penguin Group (Australia), 250 Camberwell Road, Camberwell,
Victoria 3124, Australia (a division of Pearson Australia Group Pty Ltd)
Penguin Books India Pvt Ltd, 11 Community Centre,
Panchsheel Park, New Delhi – 110 017, India
Penguin Group (NZ), 67 Apollo Drive, Rosedale, North Shore 0632,
New Zealand (a division of Pearson New Zealand Ltd)
Penguin Books (South Africa) (Pty) Ltd, 24 Sturdee Avenue,
Rosebank, Johannesburg 2196, South Africa

Penguin Books Ltd, Registered Offices:
80 Strand, London WC2R 0RL, England

First published in the United States of America by Viking Penguin,
a member of Penguin Group (USA) Inc. 2006
Published in Penguin Books 2007

1 3 5 7 9 10 8 6 4 2

PUBLISHER'S NOTE
This is a work of fiction. Names, characters, places, and incidents either are
the product of the author's imagination or are used fictitiously, and any
resemblance to actual persons, living or dead, business establishments,
events, or locales is entirely coincidental.

ISBN 0-670-03804-0 (hc.)
ISBN 978-0-14-311258-7 (pbk.)
CIP data available

Printed in the United States of America

'Behold, I will make thee a terror to thyself,
and to all thy friends.'

Jeremiah 20:4

'The terrorist and the policeman both come from
the same basket.'

Joseph Conrad, *The Secret Agent*

I

So many cases won and lost, so many small cigars smoked, so many occasions when a cold wind seemed to blow between myself and my wife, Hilda (known to me only as She Who Must Be Obeyed), so many cups of Old Bailey canteen coffee nervously consumed while waiting for a jury to come back with a verdict, so many devastating cross-examinations (the art of cross-examining is not the art of examining crossly but the gentle task of leading a witness politely into a fatal admission), so many bottles of Château Thames Embankment have come and gone since I was a white wig and sprang to fame for my conduct of the Penge Bungalow affair, in which I scored a win alone and without a leader, that sometimes I can't believe my luck in having had a life so relatively free of a dull moment.

Now my wig isn't only a darker shade of grey, it has undergone a sort of yellowing at the roots. However, I have not, thank God, been forced into any sort of retirement. I deeply pity those who have not been called to the bar. They are forced into retirement at an early age to die of boredom on some unchallenging Surrey golf course, whereas I have still kept going and am known to many as 'Rumpole of the Bailey', and can die in the wig, however yellowing, swathed in the gown, however frayed, and perform as effectively as I hope you'll agree I did during what to many people was a reign of terror.

Looking back on it now, I was, perhaps foolishly, less afraid of having a fist full of anthrax thrown in my face in Pommeroy's Wine Bar or finding our chambers in Equity Court blown up on the instructions of al-Qaeda than I was of a malignant judge or She Who Must Be Obeyed's prolonged disapproval.

It was the start of a new year and there was one disturbing fact about our home life at this period. Our mansion flat boasts three bedrooms. The largest, which I will call 'the matrimonial', is equipped to accommodate myself and She Who Must Be Obeyed in separate beds. Next to it is the guest room, prepared to receive visitors such as Dodo Mackintosh and others from Hilda's wide selection of old schoolfriends. The third, at the end of the passage, I called the 'boxroom', as it was used to accommodate bits of broken furniture, abandoned crockery, outdated telephone directories and unwanted presents from our (long-ago) wedding. There was also a stuffed elk's head from an over-grateful client, a fondue set from the Erskine-Browns for a birthday which they thought would mark my retirement and a framed quotation from the Book of Ecclesiastes presented to us by Soapy Sam Ballard, who was similarly mistaken. There was little furniture in there except an old desk, a dining chair and a camp bed, once erected for another of Hilda's schoolfriends and never folded up again.

One day, when I thought I was alone in the mansion flat, I heard noises apparently emerging from this disused room. I tried the door but found it locked. As I did so, the familiar voice of Hilda called in an exhausted and irritated tone, 'Do go away, Rumpole!' Of course I did so, but after that there were many occasions when I suspected that my wife was locked away in the boxroom. Any enquiries on the subject were met with 'Minding my own business, Rumpole, and I'd thank you to mind yours.' I didn't find out the reason for this for a long time and when I did it was not an altogether welcome revelation.

Like all the chambers in the Temple, 4 Equity Court had a list in the doorway which announced, to a criminal, adulteress or otherwise interested public, which barristers were available to help them through their troubles. As Head of Chambers, Samuel Ballard, QC, led the list, but as the oldest inhabitant Horace Rumpole's name led all the rest.

When I reported for work quite early one morning I found, to my surprise, that strips of cardboard had been stuck over this white board, quite obliterating all our names. Soapy Sam was at my heels on this occasion and I pointed it out for his explanation.

'Terrorists, Rumpole!' He spoke as though stating the obvious.

'You mean terrorists came and stuck cardboard over our names?'

'No, no. I stuck on the cardboard. Well, I asked our clerk Henry to do so.'

'May I ask with what particular end in view?'

'If the terrorists get to know that these are the chambers of a well-known barrister, let us say, one of the leaders of our profession, they might well be tempted to leave a bomb in the building. Of course, it would be a propaganda triumph for them if they were able to murder such a person.'

'It's very good of you to take such precautions on my behalf, Ballard. I may have acquired a certain notoriety through various sensational victories and a long career down the Old Bailey, or in such far-flung criminal courts as Snaresbrook and London Sessions, but I very much doubt whether al-Qaeda would think it worthwhile to launch an outrageous terrorist attack on me.'

'Oh, not on you, Rumpole. Certainly not *you*.' Soapy Sam was about to return to his usual irritating self. 'I don't suppose any terrorist would bother with a junior, however elderly and notorious, who never took silk. But blowing up a leading QC and a senior representative of our great legal system such as . . .' He seemed to be searching for a name and then remembered his own. 'Well, for instance, myself, would be a distinct feather in al-Qaeda's cap!'

'Cheer up,' I advised our leader. 'I don't suppose Bin Laden has ever heard of you. I don't believe you'd ever get a mention in the mosques of Afghanistan.'

'I don't think any of us has any idea,' Soapy Sam's smile was rigid, 'of what goes on in the terrorist's head. Now you go along in, Rumpole, and Luci Gribble will search that old portmanteau for you. We can't be too careful.'

So our fairly recently appointed Director of Marketing and Administration dug into the bag I'd bought on my earnings from the Penge Bungalow Murders and discovered a treasure trove consisting of a couple of large clean handkerchiefs, a tube of 'Suck-Us-N-C' cough sweets, a tattered copy of *The Oxford Book of English Verse* (the Quiller-Couch edition), an assortment of pens and pencils, a large notebook and the brief in *Regina* v. *Timson*, with details of Her Majesty's latest attack on yet one more member of that family.

There was another group of tireless workers who had no use for the word 'retirement'. They were the many members of that respected clan of south London villains, committing what has come to be known in this age of drugs, knifings and blackmail as 'ordinary decent crime'. There was little or no violence in the Timson records, only straightforward breaking and entering, burglary and the receiving of stolen property; unlike the Molloys, their rival family in the area, who left a trail of wounded, sometimes murdered citizens and persons dependent on exotic herbs in their wake.

I must admit, if I have to be honest, that the day-to-day financing of the Rumpole household, with Hilda's indulgence in such luxury items as furniture polish, Fairy Liquid, scrubbing brushes and Vim, would become considerably stretched if the Timson family ever did take it upon themselves to retire.

2

I took my habitual walk from Equity Court in the Temple down Fleet Street, an area greatly impoverished since all the journalists have decamped to some distant tower block. Life there seemed much as usual and there was no hint of a terrorist attack. Ludgate Circus, when I crossed it, was similarly uneventful. Then I turned off towards the familiar grey-stone building with the dome, where Justice stood, blindfolded and carrying a sword. Sometimes, I thought, she was a great deal too blindfolded for my liking and she failed to see the results of some of her wilful acts.

Then I pushed my way in through the Old Bailey doors to where a further search of myself and my bag took place, presumably to make sure I wasn't a suicide bomber. I assured the searchers I hadn't felt even the slightest temptation to commit suicide and I'd prefer my death to take place while I was wearing a wig and gown and had just completed my final speech to the jury.

In contrast to the unusual amount of searching which now went on, my appearance at that day's Timson trial was reassuringly familiar.

We were all in our usual places and Percy Timson occupied the dock. Like me, he was long past the age for retirement, but also, I suppose like me, he still couldn't resist the excitement of getting into trouble. I thought his present predicament showed a certain lowering of the

Timson standards and a loosening grip on the plot. What Percy had done, according to the prosecution, was to break and enter an empty house. It was hardly a crime for which it seemed worth the putting on of wigs and gowns, let alone occupying one of the less glamorous courts at the Old Bailey.

The prosecutor, however, thought differently and opened his case as though he was dealing with high treason, or at least the murder of the year. The Queen's case against Percy was in the slippery hands of my learned friend Colin Chertsey. He was, in fact, not at all learned or in the least bit friendly, a tall barrister with a long neck, large pointed ears and a protruding jaw who had, I thought, the personal appearance of an ill-tempered camel.

This was far from my lucky day. The case was being presided over by the judge who was often, round the Old Bailey, known as Injustice Bullingham. The facts of the case on which the Mad Bull was to be let loose were unsensational and would hardly win a place in these memoirs of mine if they didn't form a background to more extraordinary events to come.

The house at number 7, Royalty Avenue, near to Clapham Common, had been put up for sale and contained no furniture, pictures or indeed anything at all. It was this improbable venue that Percy, in his declining years, had apparently decided to break and enter by night. It seemed that Royalty Avenue had the remarkable privilege, unlike most streets in London, of having a police constable patrolling it at night. It was about two o'clock in the morning when PC Simpson saw Percy with his arm in an open window at the back of number 7.

'The prosecution will prove that Timson was entering the house for the purpose of stealing.' Chertsey of the long neck nodded his head in deep satisfaction. 'I will call a witness who will say that he heard a story current in the Needle Arms, a public house in the Camberwell area apparently frequented by the defendant and his family. This witness will say, members of the jury, that a friend told him that Percy Timson was talking about an empty house with a valuable collection of silver.'

'The witness will say no such thing.' I rose up on my hind legs to object. 'What the friend of a witness says is pure hearsay.'

'Mr Rumpole doesn't seem to be aware of the fact,' Chertsey looked condescendingly down his nose, 'that the rule against hearsay evidence has been abolished by Mr Sugden, the present Home Secretary. Your Lordship will of course have read the recent Criminal Justice Act.'

'Of course, I have it very well in mind.' The Mad Bull was protesting too much. 'We must keep up with recent developments in the law, Mr Rumpole.'

'Developments? I'd call them steps back into the Dark Ages. Whatever the new Criminal Justice Act might say, I shall tell the jury that secondhand hearsay is very unreliable evidence.'

To this the Bull said nothing, but his stubby fingers danced on the keys of the word processor with which all judges are now equipped. No doubt he was rubbishing Rumpole's submission. He then told Chertsey to carry on with his speech and my unlearned friend consulted the screen on his machine to check what he meant to say next. I was more proficient in the use of a pen and notebook, a process which seemed to me to save a lot of time.

After I had made my note, I glanced up at the public gallery. It was sparsely populated: another Timson case in an inferior court was hardly a crowd puller. But from the very front row, just above the clock, a youngish woman was smiling down at me as though I was, for her at least, an object of extraordinary interest.

'It's Tiffany, my cousin Raymond's youngest. We don't see much of Ray nowadays. She worked in a hospital and married a Paki doctor. Reckon she considers herself a cut above. What's she come here for? Just to gloat at my bit of bad luck?'

Leaning over the rails of the dock at the start of the lunchtime adjournment, Percy Timson identified my apparent fan in the public gallery. When we left the court at the end of the day the young woman whom he had called Tiffany came up to me and my solicitor, Bonny Bernard. Gloating seemed to be the last thing she had in mind.

'My whole family's always talking about you, Mr Rumpole. The way you stand up to the judges. I came to see you in action. I must say I wasn't disappointed.'

She was looking at me critically, as though still weighing me up. She was darker than most of the fairish-haired Timsons and she spoke in a way which may have caused her to be dismissed by that clan as a 'cut above'.

'Are you in trouble?' I was wondering what sort of a 'cut-above' crime she might have committed.

'Not me. It's my husband.'

'Your husband the doctor?'

'You know that?' She almost smiled for a moment, but then her voice became hushed. 'They've taken him away.

They won't tell me where. They won't tell me anything. I think it's some sort of prison.'

'What for? What do they say he's done? And who are *they* anyway?'

'The police, I suppose. I suppose that's who they were. They said they were holding him.'

'What for?'

She spoke very quietly then, as though she hardly dared speak the words. 'They said he was a terrorist.'

3

Extract from Hilda Rumpole's Memoirs

Well, at last I've done it. Gone out and bought the laptop. It was on offer at a reasonable price in Dixons, where a really helpful salesperson assured me it was an excellent buy and it would do all my spelling for me. I told him that wouldn't be necessary as I was always in the As for spelling at school.

He laughed and said I could write long letters on it, but I told him I wouldn't need it for that either. Anyway, I took it home and it fitted quite nicely into the big drawer in the old desk we keep in the boxroom.

Of course, I did all that while Rumpole was away in court, once again trying to help one of the ghastly Timson family to escape their just deserts. I can't show my laptop to Rumpole, not yet at least. He would only disapprove and give me a long lecture on the pleasures of writing with a pen. 'Much quicker,' he always says. I didn't say that my little machine would help him with his spelling, which is often eccentric, particularly when he writes in a hurry, which he always does. One day soon I suppose I'm going to have to drag Rumpole kicking and screaming into the age of new technology but not yet, not quite yet. I've got better things to do.

And I'm going to do it. I'm going to lock myself away

in the boxroom and plug in my new laptop, because I'm going to write my memoirs.

Well, I've done it. At last I've done it. I've started this journal so that at least, at some future time, people may know how things really were and what it was like to live with Rumpole night and day and particularly over the weekends, when he had no Old Bailey to go to, in Froxbury Mansions.

Rumpole writes his memoirs. Of course he does. And don't think that I don't know perfectly well that he calls me 'She Who Must Be Obeyed', as though I issued him orders instead of making suggestions to him, entirely for his own good, on such non-controversial subjects as his filthy habit of smoking small cigars which pollute the atmosphere, or staying too long on his way home in that awful little wine bar he frequents, where he spends so much on bad wine that he pleads poverty when it comes to household necessities. I never heard of a man so reluctant to pick up reasonable amounts of Vim, Fairy Liquid and J-cloths on our Saturday morning visit to Sainsbury's. Fairy Liquid is a bigger luxury than champagne in Rumpole's book.

Of course, it's all very well for Rumpole. He can put on that dirty grey wig of his, wrap himself up in that tattered old gown and step into a world that is far more exciting to him than anything that goes on in Froxbury Mansions. Ask Rumpole if he'd rather spend the afternoon with a murderer or with me helping to shell the peas and peel the potatoes, or even redecorating the bathroom, and you know perfectly well what his answer's going to be. This seems to me to be a special sort of infidelity. I don't believe Rumpole carries on with the secretaries, or even the young women barristers like that irritating Liz Probert – we all know he's not exactly Gregory Peck reborn – but it's a worse sort of infidelity in my opinion. It's hard to know that he cared more about that woman accused of poisoning her husband's beef stew than he does about someone like me, who has never even been fined for speeding.

I don't think that Rumpole completely understands this but I'm going to make it perfectly clear in my memoirs. He won't like that, of course. He probably wants me to go down in history as 'She Who Must Be Obeyed', the power-crazed, ruthless dictator of Froxbury Mansions. I suppose he'll find out eventually, whenever my memoirs get published, and I think they may come as a bit of a shock to him. So I sit in my new home while he watches the telly in the living room. The boxroom has a good strong lock to the door and Rumpole never comes in here anyway. He tried rattling the door the other day and found me in here, but of course he had absolutely no idea of what I was up to. It was just another minor eccentricity by 'She Who Must Be Obeyed'. It's the same old story. He seems to be such a good judge of who really killed who in a pub brawl in Camberwell, but he has absolutely no idea of what goes on in his own boxroom.

By the way, Rumpole has just telephoned to say that he has a conference after court and might be a bit late back. When I asked him what the conference was all about, he said he was defending a terrorist. How absolutely typical!

4

Tiffany Khan – once, somehow improbably, Tiffany Timson – sat on the edge of my client's chair in chambers as though prepared to rush off at any moment in search of the husband she seemed to believe I would have no difficulty in rescuing. As I have said, she had darker hair and eyes than the rest of the Timsons and when she spoke it was in a soft and gentle voice which I thought she might have caught, in part, from her Pakistani husband.

Her story was both simple and alarming. About twelve years ago she had got a job as a secretary at Oakwood, a north London hospital. It was there she had met Dr Khan, who was some fifteen years older than Tiffany, and they'd fallen in love, married and had two children, a boy of ten and a girl of eight.

Mahmood Khan's father had come to England in the 1970s and started a small corner shop just off the Edgware Road. His success then led to his acquiring more corner shops and he sent money back regularly to his family in Pakistan.

He also acquired a highly desirable residence, a fairly large house 'on the better side of Kilburn'. While he was living there, his wife died and his only son, Mahmood (Tiffany's husband), left Pakistan to join him in England.

Mahmood had qualified as a doctor in Pakistan but he was forced to leave the country of his birth because, Tiffany said, 'he had become involved in politics, which is a risky thing to do in Pakistan'. Tiffany wasn't at all clear what exact form her husband's politics took, but they clearly met with the outright disapproval of the Pakistan government. He told her he'd been in danger of prison, and this was when he managed to escape from his country, Tiffany said, 'by a few disguises and a long walk across the mountains', and made his way to England, where his father had organized an immigrant's visa.

In the course of time the father's businesses began to fail and he had to sell off the corner shops. That was the bad news. The good news was that Mahmood had sufficient qualifications to practise as a doctor in England and had got a post at Oakwood Hospital. It was no doubt, as Tiffany said, because Mahmood's father was so overcome with the happiness of the occasion that he had died on the night of their wedding, leaving his son the desirable house in Kilburn. Although he was permitted to remain in England and work here as a doctor, Mahmood, like his father, never became a British citizen.

There seemed to have been no blot on the contented life of the young Khan family until that dreadful morning when the police called early at the Kilburn house and Dr Mahmood met the fate he had managed to avoid in his native country. He was under arrest.

'And not being a British subject, he's liable to be deported.' Bonny Bernard spoke in pessimistic and depressing terms, a process known to him as 'preparing the client for the worst'. Tears welled in Tiffany's eyes, which she wiped quickly away with the back of her hand as she went on with her story. They came for Mahmood Khan when Tiffany was getting their children ready for school and he was about to leave for the hospital. They were three police officers in plain clothes and they refused to explain why he was being arrested or where he was being taken. He, it seemed, was controlled and told her it must be some extraordinary mistake. It was only as they were going out of the house that one of the officers thought to announce that Mahmood was being arrested under the Terrorism Act. The last thing she heard him say was that the idea was ridiculous.

'Have you any inkling why they took him?' I asked her.

'Because of what he is.' She had no doubt about it.

'You mean – a terrorist?'

'No. Pakistani. He's a Paki. That's why they're against him. All my family are against him. Never mind what sort of trouble they get into with the police, I've done the worst crime. I've married a Paki.'

'This government of ours,' I had to tell her, 'has done quite enough harm to our age-old and much-prized legal system, but I don't think it has quite got to the stage of making the fact of having been born in Pakistan a criminal offence. My solicitor, Mr Bernard, will correct me if I'm wrong.'

'Mr Rumpole's quite right,' Bonny Bernard reassured Tiffany, who clearly stood in great need of reassurance. 'We must get to know which particular brand of terrorism he's accused of.' My anxiety to comfort Tiffany had gone too far, as Bonnie Bernard was quick to point out.

'We may never know. The prosecution aren't bound to tell us anything.'

'Our present Home Secretary,' I had to inform Tiffany, 'in his wisdom, has relieved the prosecution of the trouble of making any charges at all.'

'Fred Sugden.' Bernard named the culprit, the same bright spark who had abolished the hearsay rule, to the great disadvantage of Percy Timson.

Tiffany looked puzzled, as though she hadn't entirely understood what we had told her but she was sure it wasn't good news. Then she saw a ray of hope.

'If you want someone who'll tell you Mahmood was no more a terrorist than I am, Mr Rumpole,' she said, 'there's Barry.'

'Barry who?'

'Barry Whiteside, Oakwood Hospital's administrator. They've always got on so well. He's a real friend and I never heard Barry call anyone a Paki. Anyway, he's married to a Paki like I am, Benazir. She's lovely.'

'Make a note, Bernard. We could do with a character witness.'

'He'll help Mahmood. I know he'll help him.'

'And I've got a few friends in the Home Office.' Bernard tried to sound modest about it. 'We should be able to discover where he is, at least.'

'You'll bring him back to me, Mr Rumpole?' Tiffany was looking at me with her big dark eyes full of a trust I didn't feel I had in the least deserved. 'You'll help me find Mahmood and get him out of trouble? All my family say you're wonderful in court.'

'Your family usually know what they are accused of,' I had to tell her. 'All the same, I'll do my best.'

5

Even in the reign of terror normal everyday life had to be carried on and everyday life for me consisted in cross-examining Inspector 'Persil' White, the dedicated enemy of the Timsons, an office he fulfilled in a cheerful and even occasionally friendly fashion. Encouraged by the latest attack on our legal system by the Home Secretary, he had crashed through all the restrictions of the time-honoured hearsay rule and told the jury that 'an informant' told him that Percy Timson, seated with a few friends in the snug bar of the Needle Arms, had boasted of knowing a house in Clapham where easy access through an unlocked kitchen window would lead to a treasure trove of silver and other valuable objects.

'Let me put this to you, Inspector White,' I began politely. 'Percy Timson had recently been accused of another theft, had he not?'

'You know that perfectly well, Mr Rumpole.'

'Of an offence at number 7, Grimwell Terrace, Pimlico.'

'That's the one.'

'And in that case the jury acquitted him.'

'They did.' The inspector sounded as though it was a painful memory. 'You got him off.'

'He was found not guilty.'

'Perhaps that was because he had you to defend him, Mr Rumpole.'

'Thank you, Inspector, but flattery will get you nowhere! You were annoyed at losing that case, were you not?'

'No one likes to be a loser. You must know that yourself, Mr Rumpole.'

'And being angry at your defeat, you decided to tempt Percy Timson to commit another crime?'

'What on earth do you mean by that, Mr Rumpole?' The Mad Bull assumed a puzzled expression, as though I had formed my question in some obscure foreign tongue.

'What I mean,' I said, 'and I'm sure that the jury will be quite clear about this, is that the inspector got one of his tame "informants" to discuss an empty house full of silver in the presence of Percy Timson.'

'Why on earth would I do that, Mr Rumpole?' 'Persil' White tried to look innocent.

'In order to lure Mr Timson into a crime.'

'Are you suggesting, Mr Rumpole,' the Bull had gone a deeper shade of purple and the words came effervescing out of him like the foam on a well-shaken beer bottle, 'that this officer was engaged in some dishonourable or dishonest plot?'

'It was quite understandable, My Lord. This officer, perhaps over-zealously, wanted to be in a position to arrest a man whom he thought had escaped justice. And now I'm sure the inspector will be able to answer my questions without any further assistance from Your Lordship.' And then I turned to the witness before the judicial foam could blow off the stopper. 'Inspector, Royalty Avenue in Clapham is a fairly peaceful area of London, isn't it?'

'We never had any trouble there before.'

'We all know that you rarely put a policeman on the streets nowadays.'

'It's a question of how we manage our resources, Mr Rumpole, and our resources are limited.'

'Exactly. So it would seem to be a waste of money to police a peaceful area such as Royalty Avenue.'

'As a general rule, yes.'

'As a general rule. And yet on the night Mr Percy Timson is alleged to have broken and entered there was a policeman on the street outside the house ready to catch him.'

'Sometimes we strike lucky, Mr Rumpole.'

'Sometimes we strike lucky.' The Bull ostentatiously tapped out the phrase with a heavy finger on his word processor.

'And sometimes you're cleverer than that, aren't you, Inspector? You lay the trap and wait for the suspect to fall into it. You organized a lot of talk about a hoard of silver in Royalty Avenue and kept an eye on the place until, as you hoped, Percy Timson walked into your net.'

'No, Mr Rumpole. That's not how it was at all.'

The jury, who had become interested in my cross-examination, were looking at 'Persil' White with some degree of reasonable doubt. I now had to move to the more difficult, not to say impossible, side of a defence which was weak even by Timson standards.

'My client will say that he had been to a pub in the Clapham Common area. As he was passing through Royalty Avenue, he saw the window of an empty house open and took the trouble of shutting it when he was arrested.'

Well, everyone on trial has to have their defence put

to the jury in the best possible way and I have to admit that there's no one capable of doing the job better than Rumpole. The Bull, however, in a rare moment of sanity, put the matter succinctly.

'That's what your client will say, Mr Rumpole. The question is, will the jury believe him?'

Sadly, they didn't.

'I did my best, but I'm afraid I can't hold out much hope for Percy.'

'It's not Percy we've come to see you about, Mr Rumpole.'

The speaker was Dennis, at that time the acknowledged leader of the Timson clan. Others among the group were Fred, Cyril, Tony, Jim and Doris. I had found this deputation there to greet me as I sat down to a lunch in the Old Bailey canteen while we waited for the jury to come back with a verdict.

'Not about Percy?' I was glad that they realized I was doing my best in a hopeless case. 'Then how can I help you?'

'It's not helping us we've come about,' Dennis continued in a formal and not particularly friendly way. 'It's about the help you're giving to that husband of Tiffany's.'

'We're doing our best,' I tried to reassure him. 'Of course, it's monstrous that he's never been told why he was arrested. But Mr Bernard has discovered that he's in Belmarsh Prison.'

'It's not that, Mr Rumpole.' Dennis was apparently unappeased. 'It's not that at all. The family view is, and here I speak for all of us, don't I?' This was greeted by a general nodding of Timson heads. 'We don't think you should be helping Dr Mahmood Khan at all. Not in any way, shape or form.'

'Why ever not? He's in trouble with the law. It's my duty to get him out of trouble if I possibly can. That's how I've helped every one of you from time to time.'

'With all due respect,' this time the speaker was Fred Timson, addressing me as though we were taking part in some sort of legal proceeding, 'Dr Mahmood Khan is not in the least like any of us.'

'Well, he's a doctor and he was born in Pakistan, but he's just as much entitled to a fair trial.'

'He is not like us, Mr Rumpole.' Dennis was clearly not persuaded. 'We don't blow up innocent women and children.'

'There's absolutely no evidence of that!' I protested.

'Our Will knows him.' Jim, an elderly Timson, spoke out.

'Will was courting Tiffany and he met that Paki doctor. Several occasions.'

I hadn't noticed Will among the group, but now Jim looked at a much younger man, perhaps in his thirties. Then I remembered that I had once defended Will, successfully, on a charge of post office fraud years ago. Since then he had either gone straight or avoided arrest, for he had had no further need of my services.

'I made Tiffany a fair offer. I thought so anyway.' Will seemed to find it a painful memory.

'And our Will has a lot to offer.' Fred nodded his approval. 'Own home in the Epping area. Porsche car, isn't it?'

'No, Dad.' Will smiled patiently. 'Lamborghini.'

'Anyway, him and Tiffany would have been well suited,'

Fred said. 'Except that Paki doctor was always around her. You didn't like him, did you?'

'Dishonest.' Will spoke the word as though it were a quality unknown to the Timsons. 'And he had that look in his eyes. I always suspected he might turn dangerous.'

'Terrorism. Isn't that what they've got him for?' Fred was triumphant.

'That's what they've said, but we have no idea what sort of evidence they've got.'

'I think we've come to a decision, Mr Rumpole.' Dennis Timson, like those who arrested Tiffany's husband, seemed uninterested in the question of evidence. 'We don't want to see you sticking up for a Paki terrorist.'

'We don't know yet if he is a terrorist.' I tried to remain reasonably calm. 'Anyway, you know I'm just an old taxi. If a client flags me down, I'm bound to give them a ride. To the best of my ability.'

'If you defend him,' Dennis ignored my speech, 'we have agreed we will have to look elsewhere if anyone of the name of Timson is in need of a legal brief. Do I express the view of the meeting?'

At this the various Timson heads nodded in agreement. It was, I reluctantly understood, their way of saying goodbye.

6

Extract from Hilda Rumpole's Memoirs

'I tried to explain to the Timsons that I'm just an old taxi.'

This is what Rumpole said. I felt like telling him that all those years ago, when he was a pupil in Daddy's chambers, I really had no intention of marrying an old taxi. In fact I had higher hopes for him. I saw a future with Rumpole, QC, or one with Mr Justice Rumpole. Of course, it wasn't to be, mainly because of the quality of the riff-raff he took for rides in that old taxi of his.

Of course, Rumpole does have a better type of client occasionally, people with decent homes and proper jobs, the sort of people you might enjoy meeting for lunch at Harrods, say, or Fortnum and Mason. But then Rumpole meets such people when it's a case of a husband murdering his wife, or vice versa. And I know I shouldn't say this, but when it comes to wives murdering their husbands, I can sort of feel some sympathy for them on occasion. I haven't been married to Rumpole all these years without finding out how really irritating husbands can be from time to time, and particularly now.

Not serious, of course, with regard to the above. I'd have to stop short of murder; but I'm not quite sure how I can express my frustration at the way he's behaving now.

In the absence of the better class of client, Rumpole came to depend on that terrible family of hardened villains, the Timsons, or whatever they choose to call themselves. Rumpole always says we can rely on them to provide us with what we need to buy at the Saturday morning shop at Sainsbury's. And now it seems he's fallen out with even *them*. They've told him they're going to look elsewhere for their legal representation, and all because of the last client he's chosen to open his old taxi door to – a terrorist!

To be honest, I have to say I fully understand the terrible Timsons' views on this subject. I think, and I'm sure most decent people in the country think, that terrorists don't need defending. What they need is locking up securely, or at least turfing out of the country.

It seems to me sometimes that Rumpole takes a sort of perverse delight in disagreeing with what ordinary decent people think. He thinks that defending this terrorist is as good as the really important property cases Daddy used to do so brilliantly. He's going to put all his energy into defending him, quite regardless of what anyone else thinks about it.

It all started when he met the terrorist's wife. 'Eyes full of tears like dark pools full of water' was how he put it to me over supper when he'd almost come to the end of his usual bottle of Pommeroy's plonk. Well, all I can say is, a lot of terrorists may have wives with eyes like deep pools, but that doesn't make it any the less urgent to lock them up or turf them out with no unnecessary delay. And for all Rumpole knows about it, their wives may also be implicated, right up to their pool-like eyes.

As I sit here in the boxroom writing, I can only report

that my dear old schoolfriend Dodo Mackintosh is coming for a few days to do the sales, so I'll have an ally to help me through this worst of times.

And to cap it all, he has just announced that a conference has been fixed with his miserable terrorist in Belmarsh Prison and he's got to turn up there with his passport. He couldn't be more excited if he'd been invited to tea with the Queen in Windsor Castle, but that's Rumpole all over, isn't it?

7

Perhaps there aren't any particularly nice prisons, not one you'd want to spend a relaxing year or two in, but Belmarsh is certainly to be avoided. It occupies a large, flat area by the Thames known as Plumstead Manor and is connected to Woolwich Court, so an invited person can be shut into it after a trial without necessarily coming up for air. The exercise yard is covered over, in case helicopters should swoop down and rescue the particularly important inmates. The result of this is those in custody never see what Oscar Wilde called 'that little tent of blue which prisoners call the sky'.

Getting to Belmarsh by public transport would entail a train and a bus ride or a bus ride and a walk, so Bonny Bernard offered to drive me in his family car. It was an offer I couldn't refuse.

Now, in his professional life Bernard is a wise and careful fellow, perhaps more unlikely than I am to take risks, but at the wheel of the Mondeo he became a different character, accelerating as though on a racetrack, hooting and muttering insults at other, more reasonably paced drivers.

Not only was there the element of danger, the drive did not exactly pass through beautiful countryside. We headed east from the Temple, along the Commercial Road, and drove through the Blackwall Tunnel under the river, then along the Woolwich Road to Plumstead, past gaunt and unappealing buildings, to the new prison, built in the 1990s, which resembles, architecturally, the supermarket Hilda and I visit on Saturday mornings.

Belmarsh is a maximum-security prison which houses murderers, rapists and major drug barons. The visitors' centre, where we had to check in, was crowded with their friends and relatives. After a considerable wait we were asked to show our passports, empty our pockets of everything except one pen each and surrender our fingers to some form of invisible ink. These prolonged formalities gave me the feeling of entering another country, a land in which the principles of justice had been forgotten.

From the visitors' centre it was a ten-minute walk to the prison, where we were searched again and had our fingers inspected. I was also relieved of a lever-arch file which would eventually contain my notes of the conference with Mahmood Khan. The file was examined with deep suspicion by the authorities, who apparently thought it could be used by my client to tunnel his way out of custody, or at least become a weapon of mass destruction. We were sent back to hand it in at our first port of call. At last Bonny Bernard and I were installed in an interview room to wait, for what seemed an unusually long time, for the delivery of our client.

There had been some developments since Tiffany called for our help in the corridor of the Old Bailey. The indefatigable Bernard had issued an appeal to SIAC, the Special Immigration Appeals Commission. The powers that be, it seemed, understood that Dr Khan could not be sent back to Pakistan as he'd be at risk of being subject to torture and imprisonment because of his 'political activities' in that far-off country. They therefore offered him the alternative delight of being locked up in Belmarsh for an indefinite period of time.

Some sort of preliminary statement of a case had been served on Bonny Bernard. It merely told us that information had been received that Dr Khan was regularly in touch with a terrorist organization in London with whom he corresponded. He had, the statement went on, encouraged, helped and suggested acts of terrorism. Names, dates, places and circumstances relied on were notably absent from this document.

At last our client was brought to us in an interview room, by which time I was exhausted by the unusual exercise and resentful at the exclusion of my lever-arch file. By contrast, Mahmood Khan seemed composed and even, extraordinarily enough, moderately cheerful. He was small, I thought not much taller than his wife. He also had large brown eyes and they were filled, not with tears, but with a look of incredulous amusement at the extraordinary situation in which he found himself. He sat on one of the four hard chairs the room contained, his hands neatly folded on his lap, and he looked at me as though I was just another inexplicable surprise that fate had inflicted on him.

'My name's Horace Rumpole,' I told him. 'I am a criminal barrister. That is,' I was anxious not to be misunderstood, 'I am a barrister who does criminal cases. I'm pretty well known. You might, perhaps, have heard of me.'

'No, Mr Rumpole. I'm afraid I have not heard of you. Should I have?'

'It doesn't matter,' I hastened to reassure him. 'And this is Mr Bernard, the solicitor who is also prepared to act for you.' (I didn't add, 'You certainly won't have heard of him.') 'Your wife came to meet us down at the Old Bailey and asked us to take on your case.'

'My wife. Yes. This must be very hard for her. And the children, of course. They must be completely mystified.'

'The government wants to keep you here,' I told him, 'because it would be unsafe for you to return to Pakistan. Apparently you were plotting there, against the regime.'

'Oh, we wanted to do *terrible* things, Mr Rumpole. We wanted women's rights and free speech and fair trial and police who didn't do things like strangle a woman's baby to make her confess. In fact, we wanted all the good things you have in England. So naturally if I went back they would apply electronic charges to various parts of my body and lock me up.' Dr Khan's smile widened. 'You see, I freely confess my guilt.'

Bonny Bernard was regarding our client with obvious admiration, and I was conscious that he had come, so far, better out of the interview than his somewhat hesitant defender. All the same I had to return to the business in hand.

'You read a copy of the notice served on Mr Bernard?'

'Yes, indeed.' Dr Khan managed to look as though he was enjoying the joke. 'I'm meant to have been involved in a plot to blow up London.'

'Is there any truth in that at all?'

'Of course not. How could there be?'

'Do you know anyone who talks to you about terrorism in England? Anyone who says they approve of it?'

'If they did I would immediately end the conversation. I, who love England, have an English wife, my children go to English schools. I, who have spent the best part of my life here. England is my home, my dear, dear country.'

'You don't have to go that far.' I felt the good doctor was rather over-egging the pudding. 'I mean, it's not compulsory to respect the royal family, eat roast beef and care deeply about cricket.'

'Oh, but I do, Mr Rumpole. Indeed I do.' My unexpected client still seemed to be on the verge of laughter. 'I have a huge respect for Her Majesty. Tiffany can cook excellent roast beef. And I often take my boy to watch the cricket at Lord's. That is, whenever I get a day off from the hospital.'

It was all too good to be entirely true: the amused stoicism, the enthusiasm for England which anyone English would find embarrassing. Wouldn't an innocent man have boiled over with anger, raged against the authorities, damned the police and showed nothing but contempt for a country which had arbitrarily imprisoned him? Would any innocent man treat the whole affair as though it was an unfortunate but slightly amusing collapse of a number of wickets?

Such thoughts occurred to me but I suppressed them. It was my job to argue his case as well as it could be argued. I just hoped that he would stop behaving like David Niven in some ancient film of understated wartime heroism.

'Have you any enemies?' I went on to ask, as usual suppressing my possible disbelief. 'People who might have informed the police against you?'

'Enemies?' Trying hard to think, Mahmood was feeling the back of his neck. 'I don't think so. Tiffany's family don't like me very much, but that hasn't landed me in prison, has it?'

'Probably not. There's only one way to flush a bit of information out of the powers that be then. We're going to appeal against your detention. Then we might get some clue as to what this is all about. Mr Bernard will tell you about the procedure.' I hoped our client wouldn't guess that I was moving into unfamiliar territory.

'We're going before the Special Immigration Appeals Commission,' Bernard explained. 'It's chaired by a judge and heard in the law courts. You can be represented there by the counsel of your choice. I assume that will be Mr Rumpole, whom you have now met.'

'Mr Rumpole, of course.' Our client sounded enthusiastic. 'Now I remember the name. I have read it often in the newspapers. I know that you, Mr Rumpole, are a great fighter for the truth in the Courts of Law.'

'We can only hope,' I told him, 'that SIAC will turn out to be a Court of Law.'

8

Claude Erskine-Brown, the opera-loving, inferior advocate, the frequently love-torn member of our chambers, came striding confidently into my room and lowered himself into my client's chair and asked, 'Aren't you going to congratulate me, Rumpole?'

'You've managed to win a case?'

'A good many. But it's not that.'

'You've found the love of your life?'

I asked the question with a sinking of the heart. Claude was married to a High Court judge, Dame Phillida Erskine-Brown, who had been, in happier days, my pupil Phillida Trant, later to become the Portia of our chambers. She bore Claude two children, Tristan and Isolde, named after his operatic favourites. On her becoming a scarlet judge, she treated me with unusual severity, no doubt in order to prove to the world that having once been my pupil she was not going to do me any favours. The stability of this marriage had survived the many occasions when Claude conceived a desperate passion for some client, court official, lady barrister or, on one famous occasion, the Home Secretary. These affairs of the heart were, in Claude's case, about as successful as one of his cross-examinations.

'Well, out with it,' I said, hoping to get the confessional over quickly. 'Who are you in love with today?'

'Love?' He spoke as though it were a matter of which he had little or no experience. 'This is a serious matter, Rumpole, and I take it as a great honour. I have received an appointment.'

My mind boggled. The idea of Mr Justice Claude was clearly ridiculous. No Lord Chancellor with even the most superficial knowledge of Claude could have made such an appointment.

'Is it the Weights and Measures Committee?' I asked in good faith.

'No, Rumpole. It is not Weights and Measures. I have been appointed a counsel to SIAC.'

I heard once again the brief hiccup of disgust Bonny Bernard had uttered in Belmarsh Prison.

'How very convenient. I've got the case of a Dr Khan. He's appealing to your commission.'

'Then I shall see that the court appreciates any points there might be in his favour.'

'No need for that.'

'That will be my job, Rumpole.' Claude spoke with obvious pride and satisfaction.

'I mean, I will be there to argue the case.'

'Will you?' This was said with a distinct note of disappointment. 'It won't really be necessary. I am the lawyer appointed by the court to see that your client is treated according to his deserts.'

'"Use every man after his desert and who would 'scape whipping?"' I was sure that Claude did not recognize the quotation from *Hamlet*, so I made my position entirely clear. 'I'm the lawyer appointed by Dr Khan to see that his case is put as well as it can possibly be.' ('And far better than you would ever be able to do it,' was what I didn't add.)

'You're entitled to be there.' Claude said this, I thought, a little grudgingly.

'If your commission's entitled to keep a man locked up in prison, of course I'm entitled to be there. And while I'm about it, would you mind giving me further and better particulars of the charges against Dr Khan?'

'You've had a general statement.'

'Worthless! All it says is that someone suspects him of being involved in a terrorist plot.'

'Not just someone, Rumpole. The Home Secretary.'

'To my mind that makes the situation rather worse. Places, dates, times? When and where and with whom was he involved?'

'I can't tell you that, Rumpole.'

'But you know.'

'As a friend of the court, I shall be completely informed. But I won't be allowed to broadcast such facts, either in chambers or in court. Government sources have to be protected.'

'I thought you were there to protect Dr Khan.'

'From what I've heard of him, I suspect he knows all about the where and the when and a lot more besides.'

'I'll see you in court, Erskine-Brown,' I said to avoid further argument. 'And I'll apply for further and better particulars of any crime anyone thinks Dr Khan may have committed.'

In all honesty I can't say that those months marked the happiest or the most successful period of the Rumpole career. For a start the mansion flat had to accommodate a prolonged visit from Hilda's old schoolfriend Dodo Mackintosh. This Dodo, whose indifferent watercolours of Lamorna Cove failed to cheer up our living room, had formed the view, from what Hilda had told her about the Khan case, that I was a fully paid-up member of al-Qaeda.

'This Dr Khan.' Dodo seemed to have appointed herself a member of the prosecution. 'He's not a British citizen, is he?'

'He's lived here for twenty-odd years. He didn't think he had to go through the business of becoming a citizen.'

'He could always have gone back to Afghanistan or wherever it was.'

'Pakistan.'

'Then why didn't he go there?' Hilda joined her old schoolfriend in the argument.

'Because he'd be arrested and probably tortured. He was in a group working against the government.'

'So he was a terrorist there too, was he?' Dodo asked the question with quizzically raised eyebrows and in a manner which I found particularly irritating.

'So far as I know, his protests were entirely peaceful.'

'The trouble with people like your Dr Khan,' Dodo spoke confidently, as though she had studied my instructions from Bonny Bernard clearly, 'is that they don't want to take on the British way of life. They simply don't understand our values.'

'Understand our values?' I repeated. 'It may surprise you to know that Dr Khan is devoted to the royal family, roast beef and cricket. In that respect he's a great deal more English than I am.'

'What do you mean, Rumpole?' Dodo asked the question with a sigh.

'At school I was never devoted to cricket. Every time

they shouted, "Over", I moved further and further away from the action until, in the end, I was lying in the long grass, reading detective stories.'

'Rumpole always tried to be different,' Hilda explained to her friend. 'Even when he was a schoolboy.'

It was evening in the mansion flat, in the long hours between supper and bedtime, and my fingers were itching to turn on the news. I searched for an accommodating statement which would put an end to the conversation.

'I may be ridiculously old-fashioned,' I said, 'but I prefer to believe Dr Khan is innocent until he's proved guilty.'

'I think,' Dodo Mackintosh, the watercolour artist from Cornwall, told me, 'you really are very old-fashioned about most things, Rumpole.'

She and Hilda went off together shortly after that and I was able to watch the news. Later I heard the sound of jovial laughter issuing from the boxroom.

Things were little better in chambers. Luci, with an 'i', Gribble cheerfully told me that my terrorist practice wasn't going to do anything for chambers 'image-wise', and couldn't I find myself a nice sensational murder to get me back in the tabloids? Soapy Sam Ballard called on me in person to advise me to dump the Khan case. 'We already have the excellent news of Claude Erskine-Brown being appointed to argue the justice of the case as adviser to the court.'

'And you don't object to that?'

'A more personal contact with a terrorist by a member of chambers, however long in call and approaching the end of his career, would really single us out as a legal bolthole for some of the most dangerous clients in the world today.'

'You mean, word will go round the souks of Saudi Arabia and Iran that as soon as you've blown up the Houses of Parliament, you should make straight for 4 Equity Court?'

Ballard didn't immediately answer my question. Instead he looked thoughtfully into the middle distance. Then he said, 'Peter Plaistow, QC, MP, prosecutes in most of these cases. You know Plaistow, of course?'

'Never heard of the fellow,' I had to confess.

'Charming chap, Rumpole. Perfectly charming. Peter's right at the heart of New Labour. Of course, he has the ear of the Home Secretary.'

'I shouldn't think that's a particularly attractive thing to have.'

'And he's very close to the Lord Chancellor,' Ballard ignored my comment. 'No doubt he exerts a good deal of influence when it comes to the question of appointing judges.'

'Are you thinking of getting your bottom on the bench?' I'm afraid I was rude enough to ask.

'I'm not speaking of myself exactly.' Ballard's smile was still irritatingly tolerant. 'I'm thinking of Equity Court in general. We hardly want to get the reputation of being a thorn in the flesh of the government, do we, Rumpole?'

'Don't you, Ballard? Speaking for myself, I can think of no finer reputation.' At which our Head of Chambers gave me an even sadder look and left quietly, as though leaving a person suffering from a serious, and probably fatal, disease.

*

The only person who seemed able to approach the Khan case as simply another brief in another potential miscarriage of justice was my old friend and loyal, trustworthy solicitor, Bonny Bernard.

He discovered the date when Dr Khan's case was likely to come up before the curiously named SIAC. Barrington Whiteside, the hospital administrator, was prepared to tell us all he knew about Dr Khan, but he preferred to do so at an informal meeting as he had to clear things with Oakwood before he would be allowed to give evidence. I took the phrase 'informal meeting' to mean a chat over a bottle of Château Thames Embankment at the corner table in Pommeroy's Wine Bar and arrangements were made accordingly.

I have to say that I took immediately to Barry Whiteside. He was a large grey-haired man with a twinkle in his eye which reassuringly indicated that he didn't take many things in life, including himself, too seriously. After we had settled down and Barry Whiteside further endeared himself to me by insisting on stumping up for the bottle of Pommeroy's plonk, he became suddenly serious.

'As I've tried to explain to Tiffany here,' he said, 'the idea of her husband being engaged in any illegal activity, let alone terrorism, is simply ridiculous.'

The ever-anxious Tiffany had come with Whiteside to the meeting. She looked so beautiful that I doubted whether she was pure Timson; surely she was the result of some more exotic misalliance, a moment of infidelity, perhaps, by her mother. Her pool-like eyes were no longer filled with tears but shone with gratitude as the hospital administrator further endorsed her husband.

'Of course, there is racial prejudice in Oakwood, as there is everywhere else, but I can't tolerate it myself. Mahmood's a first-rate doctor, whether he comes from Pakistan or Perivale. Of course, I might be a bit prejudiced in favour of "Pakis", seeing that I married one myself.'

'The beautiful Benazir,' Tiffany told us. 'She's lovely.'

'We've all four been friends for years.'

'Really? Then tell us a bit more about your friend Dr Khan.'

I got, as I expected, a good report, but no more light thrown on the terrorist charges.

'An excellent doctor,' Barry told me, 'but I'm sure you know that. And a deeply caring man. We're very keen on relative support at Oakwood. So many hospitals spend no time with worried relatives and get rid of them as soon as possible. But we turned an old house in the hospital grounds into a Relatives' and Visitors' Centre. They can wait there and rest, get cups of tea and be told about the hospital and their loved ones' problems. Mahmood started a Muslim room there. We have so many in our catchment area and Mahmood often talks to relatives personally. He has a desk down there and a sort of filing system. I don't know how he copes with all he does, I honestly don't.'

'Did you feel there were any mysteries in Dr Khan's life?' I asked Barry.

'You mean, might he have been a secret terrorist?'

'Something like that, yes.'

'Absolutely ridiculous!' Barry told me. 'Mahmood is completely crazy about England.'

'He is more English than the English,' Tiffany said. 'He always stands up to attention when they play the National

Anthem. Always wears a poppy on Armistice Day. We have turkey and listen to the Queen on Christmas Day.'

'He even loves the English weather,' Barry told me. 'He said they never got gentle rain in Pakistan. He said he was so proud of what he called "owning property in England".'

'Our home,' Tiffany told me with serious pleasure.

'A splendid house,' Barry assured me. 'Right on the sunny side of Kilburn. It's really Queen's Park. Benazir and I slum it down at the wrong end. We try not to show how jealous we are!'

'Barry and Benazir are such good friends to us.' Tiffany sounded happy for a moment. 'We were always in and out of each other's houses.'

'Let's talk about your husband.' I had to bring the attention of the meeting away from the happy past to the nightmare of Dr Khan's present. 'Did you notice anything, anything at all, unusual in the week, let's say the month, before he was arrested?'

After a moment, Tiffany said, 'He said he thought he was being followed. He said that once or twice. I'm not quite sure how he got the idea.'

'When was that?'

'Last year. We went away for a holiday just before Christmas. It was after that.'

'Did he say who was following him?'

'No. Just that there'd be a man and he'd get off a bus or whatever just after he did. Sometimes he turned round, but the man had managed to disappear.'

'Was it always the same man?'

'It only happened four or five times. But it was the same man, yes.'

'Did he say why he thought anyone would follow him?'

'Yes.' Tiffany smiled. 'He thought they were pestering him to buy more raffle tickets for the hospital ball. He made a joke of it.'

'He always made a joke of things,' Barry agreed. 'He thought that was typically English. Now, to get back to business, do you think you'd like me as a character witness?'

'I think we'd love you as a character witness,' I assured him.

It turned out there were certain formalities to be gone through with the hospital authorities, certain permissions to be granted or refused. 'But whatever they say, even if they cut up rough, you can count on me being there, Mr Rumpole. I'm not letting Mahmood down.'

As I was thanking Barry, another member of our chambers, a man called Hoskins, who complained a good deal about the number of briefs he needed to meet the expense of supporting several, I forget how many, daughters, passed our table. He called out in a loud voice, 'Congratulations, Rumpole. You've got a remarkably pretty girl having drinks with you.'

'Who on earth was that?' Tiffany asked, understandably affronted.

'It's a man called Hoskins,' I told her. 'And I'm not sure that I like him very much. Or indeed at all.'

9

Extract from Hilda Rumpole's Memoirs

It's been a joy having Dodo here, being able to stay up late remembering not only our schooldays, but so much that has happened since. Dodo has always been friendly and helpful to Rumpole, going so far as preparing cheesy bits for parties in chambers whenever she is up here and available.

However, I don't think I can get Rumpole to *like* Dodo. It's not that he's ever been rude to her. He wouldn't dare. But Rumpole loves to be the centre of attention around the mansion flat. It's *his* cases we are always discussing, the way *he* managed to get the better of Judge Bullingham, for instance, or the time at which *he* got up to polish off his final speech, or the long conference that was going to make *him* late home for supper. Above all else Rumpole likes to talk and he doesn't like having to sit there and listen to what Dodo and I have to say about *our* old friends and the things we got up to when we were all at school together. He might be a great performer in court, but he's not much of an audience at home.

Laura Hoskins goes to my bridge club. Peter Hoskins, Laura's husband, is, as it happens, in Rumpole's chambers. They have four daughters, aged fifteen to twenty-two, which runs the Hoskinses into a good deal of expense. Well, although Peter always comes home as quickly as possible from chambers, it seems that only a week ago he was invited into that dingy wine bar, Pommeroy's, and he reported to his wife that he'd spotted Rumpole in there drinking with a remarkably pretty girl with big brown eyes with whom he was obviously smitten.

Of course I remembered he'd chatted about a female client with eyes like dark pools full of tears. It seems she wasn't so tearful in the wine bar, but no doubt flattered by Rumpole's attentions, even though he is far too old for even the mildest sort of flirtation. However, Dodo took it more seriously. She'd been in touch recently with Maggie Parvine, who was a bit of a star at school, and she said that Maggie's husband, Richard, who was almost as old as Rumpole, was suffering from the same sort of thing, inviting young girls out to drinks and making up to them.

Well, it seems that Maggie consulted her extremely good local GP in Basingstoke and he said it was a health hazard. As men grow older their willpower, and the instincts which make them behave sensibly, grow weaker. He'd seen it happen with dozens of patients – MPs, headmasters, chairmen of companies, even clerics, they simply needed, well, as Maggie's GP said it, something to strengthen both body and mind, and he put Maggie's husband on a course of Omni Vite, a preparation of amounts of vitamins and natural remedies. It's become clear to me that in many ways Rumpole is losing his grip. So we have decided to put him on a course of Omni Vite which merely consists of taking a small drink, night and morning.

Of course, he's being extremely difficult about taking it regularly. He starts off talking rubbish about 'eye of newt and toe of frog' and 'slivered in the moon's eclipse'. At first he refused the drinks altogether, until I made it clear that I would leave him and live in Cornwall with Dodo, taking him to the cleaners as far as alimony was concerned. He was also not to make a face as he drank it. We had tried the Omni Vite and, as Dodo said, 'It tasted of all the goodness of the earth.' If we're watching, he knows he has to drink it, but as soon as our backs are turned I know he gets up to tricks such as pouring it away in a plant pot, or on one occasion into a half-empty teapot.

Rumpole is determined to win the appeal of that ghastly terrorist who is now safely in Belmarsh Prison. This is absolutely the right place for Dr Mahmood Khan, if you want my opinion, or that of most sensible people, but when I tell Rumpole this he starts talking about Magna Carta and the Bill of Rights. And he hardly listens when I tell him that there were no suicide bombers and no al-Qaeda when King John signed up to the charter on the island of Runnymede.

So all I can do is tell Rumpole that if he doesn't take his Omni Vite regularly I'm leaving home.

10

'I've had a talk with your hospital administrator, Barrington Whiteside.'

'A thoroughly decent chap, Barry. One of the best,' Dr Khan told me.

'I'm inclined to agree with you.'

Once again Bonny Bernard and I had passed, with the usual difficulties and prolonged questions, into that strange foreign country which was Belmarsh Prison. And now we were closeted with our client, who once again looked neat, smiling and inexplicably relaxed.

'I understand that you complained of being followed in the street. Why didn't you tell me that?'

'It might have been my imagination. It didn't seem important.'

'Everything that's happened to you recently is important. Was it always the same man or men following you?'

'I thought it might be the same man. I only got a glance at him.'

'How many times? More than once?'

'Perhaps four or five times. I'd get off the bus and he'd be on the pavement behind me. I'd look back and he'd be gone. Or I'd go into a shop and find someone I'd vaguely noticed before standing outside the door. I don't suppose it's important, is it, Mr Rumpole?'

'We don't know what's important yet. Has anything

unusual happened to you? Anything you couldn't explain at the time?'

'Not really. Only when I got sent to the wrong address. It was a silly mistake, I suppose.'

'What happened?'

'I got a text message from Mrs Bina Singh. She'd gone through quite a serious cancer operation and I looked after her on her regular visits to the hospital. She wanted to meet me urgently at her home at twelve-thirty the next day. It was an address in Willesden. I tried ringing her on the number the hospital had, but there was no reply. So I decided to call at the Willesden house.'

'When was this?'

'Earlier this year. January, I think it was.'

'So what happened when you got to the house?'

'It was the wrong address. I rang the bell and a man from Pakistan answered it. There were two other men in the hall. They were very rude, Mr Rumpole. Very ill-mannered. They wanted to know who I was, who sent me. I tried to explain but I don't think they believed me. It was clear that Mrs Singh had nothing to do with the place. In the end they pushed me out of the door. Warned me never to come to the place again. It was a bit odd.'

'I would say so. Did you speak to Mrs Singh after that?'

'Naturally. She said she never texted me. She wouldn't have known how to do such a thing. It was all a bit of a joke really.'

'Not a particularly funny one. What was the address?'

'Highfield Road. I forget the number.'

'Did you ever go back there?'

'Just once. Out of curiosity. The place was boarded up,

with a "For Sale" notice.' He gave a little laugh. 'It was all a ridiculous mistake.'

Once again he was doing his act as a typical stoic, or perhaps a not very bright Englishman. And once again the act seemed artificial and unconvincing. Was it all a disguise, and a particularly effective one? Had he, in fact, been rightly arrested as a terrorist? I allowed my disbelief a little while to speculate and then shut it up again in the cupboard.

'Do you travel to work by bus?' I asked him.

'Only sometimes. When Tiffany needs the car.'

'Did you tell Tiffany about being followed?'

'I mentioned it to her but I made a joke of it by saying I thought someone was trying to sell me raffle tickets for a hospital dance.'

'Why did you say that?'

'I was so uncertain and I didn't want to worry her.' And then Dr Khan gave one of his patiently amused smiles and said, 'It doesn't make sense at all, does it?'

'At some point,' I told my client, 'we'll have to make sense of it. In the meantime, I've got to make sense of this strange commission.'

11

'Eye of newt and toe of frog, Wool of bat and tongue of dog.'

'Don't forget your Omni Vite today of all days, Rumpole, now that you're actually appearing in court.'

She Who Must had exercised her usual talent of raising two unpleasant matters in the course of a single sentence. One was the question of the repulsive medicine she and her friend Dodo were forcing me to take, a horrid distillation smelling of rotting parsnips dipped in seaweed in which I could identify all the ingredients mentioned by the witches in *Macbeth*, including the pilot's thumb. She had also touched on a further sore point. It was true that I had hardly been busy or much engaged in court during the past months: the withdrawal of their patronage by the Timson family had made an appreciable hole in the Rumpole bank account.

I sniffed the Omni Vite and shuddered at the familiar smell.

'Drink it down, Rumpole. You know what good it's doing you.' Hilda was standing over me. I had no alternative but to swallow it.

'That wasn't too bad, was it?'

'All I can say is that the witches seem to have added an extra lizard's leg to the brew.'

'Try not to be ridiculous. Off you go and, by the way,

Dodo and I both think that terrorist of yours should stay in prison. Best place for him, Dodo thinks.'

'Then it'll come as something of a relief not to have your friend Dodo on the bench,' was what I didn't say. Instead I took a swig of tea to wash down the last of the Omni Vite and cleanse the gullet. Then I left for work.

From the Temple I only had to cross Fleet Street to reach the Law Courts, the huge, sham Gothic château on the Strand that houses innumerable courts as well as a mosaicked hall where the secretaries emerge to play badminton in the evening (or so the rumour goes). In no other part of the building to my knowledge have the fundamental principles of British justice been forgotten or indefinite imprisonment without charge been approved of. I hoped that these great traditions would rub off on the mysterious commission.

These hopes were a little dashed when I met the prosecuting counsel and rising star of the New Labour Party. This was Peter Plaistow, a tall, winsome barrister with chestnut hair which peeped discreetly out from under his wig. He was surrounded, outside the court, by a posse of civil servants, which I had to penetrate to approach the Prime Minister's favourite QC.

'My name's Rumpole,' I gave it to him straight. 'And I'm against you in the Khan case.'

'Oh, my dear,' Peter Plaistow affected a look of mock terror, 'I hope you're not going to attack me viciously. Everyone tells me you're absolutely ruthless down at the Old Bailey.'

'That's as may be.' I can't say I didn't feel flattered by

this alleged reputation. 'I haven't seen you much, round the Old Bailey.'

'No. I avoid it as much as possible. I'm sure you'll find this a perfectly friendly court.'

'Good! I'm glad to hear it.'

'Is there any way I can help you, before we all "go into battle"?' He spoke the last three words in inverted commas, as though he didn't really expect us to have any arguments at all.

'There certainly is,' I told him. 'I want further and better particulars.'

'Particulars?' he asked, as though I had uttered a word in a strange language.

'Yes. Particulars of the case against my client. Dates, places, times. Details of what he's supposed to have done. When, where and with whom. You must know what "particulars" are, from a thousand other cases.'

'In other cases, yes.' Plaistow was smiling more charmingly than ever. 'But here in SIAC we don't "do" particulars. Your client knows that we received information about his terrorist activities.'

'Yes. But what sort of activities? Are we ever going to know that?'

'My dear, I'm so sorry.' Plaistow appeared genuinely sympathetic. 'But there's this rather cheery chap, Erskine-Brown I believe his name is. He will put your case fairly before the court.'

'Is he going to give me the particulars?'

'I'm afraid not. But you can rely on Erskine-Brown to argue any sort of defence your client may have.'

'To rely on Erskine-Brown to put my defence,' I had to tell the elegant MP, 'is like relying on a bobbin of darning wool to pull you up the side of a mountain.'

Undeterred, I now approached the newly appointed Erskine-Brown and found him surrounded by a similar bunch of Home Office officials. He was chatting with them in what was for him a fairly animated sort of way.

'I don't want to interrupt the conversation, Claude,' I told him, 'but Peter Plaistow over there told me that you were the chap who'd give me particulars of the charges against my client.' The civil servants round Claude looked shocked and he appeared incredulous.

'You're trying it on, aren't you, Rumpole?' he suggested.

'Trying what on?' I did my best to look innocent.

'Peter Plaistow told you nothing of the sort. He knows perfectly well that we don't do further particulars here at SIAC.'

'So you don't "do" fair trials then?'

'Of course it'll be fair! You know, Rumpole, I'll see to that.'

I didn't say I couldn't trust Claude to tell the difference between a fair trial and the proceedings of the Spanish Inquisition. Instead I said, 'It's the first principle of British justice that the accused should know what he's charged with. Don't you remember that from your student days, when you read *Criminal Law for Beginners*? If you won't tell me I'll have to apply to the court.'

As I walked off, my confidence fuelled by anger, I noticed that Claude's rabble of civil servants no longer looked appalled. They were now quietly amused.

Mrs Justice Templett had sat on the bench for many years, in fact she was appointed when there were not nearly as many women judges as there are today. On her elevation she seemed to feel it right to suppress any feminine qualities that might cause controversy. She wore no make-up, although it was said that she allowed herself a thin line of lipstick when trying murder cases. Her first name, which was Floribel, was kept strictly under wraps, never to be referred to. She behaved with particular severity towards any woman unfortunate enough to appear before her in a divorce or criminal case.

She was flanked by other members of the commission who seemed to have been placed there merely as book-ends, or to decorate the otherwise sparsely populated courtroom, because Floribel Templett gave them little opportunity to intervene in the proceedings.

On the other side of the court sat Peter Plaistow, QC, MP, and Claude Erskine-Brown, who looked almost unbearably self-satisfied at having to take part in important affairs of state. They were flanked by the Home Office officials and lawyers who had given them, no doubt, their little brief authority.

On the other side, I was in the second row, and behind me Dr Khan sat informally with my faithful solicitor, a small enough band to fight the assembled powers of the state.

'Mr Rumpole,' Floribel turned a vaguely disapproving eye on my good self, 'we understand you have some sort of an application to make.'

'Indeed I have, My Lady. And it's not some sort of an application. It's an application which concerns our civil rights, our liberties and the basic principles of our criminal law.'

'Very well.' Her Ladyship sighed heavily and looked at me as though I were some woman taken in adultery or had at least been caught pinching knickers in Marks and Spencer. 'You may make your point shortly.'

'I can put it very shortly. Dr Khan is at least entitled to know what the charges are against him. That he should be denied that right is unthinkable. That's all I have to say.'

'Is it really, Mr Rumpole? You're not normally at a loss for words.'

At this the bookends giggled obediently. Peter Plaistow smiled and Claude permitted himself a quiet guffaw.

'Very well. If Your Ladyship wants further argument I am quite prepared for it.' During the next half an hour I trundled the old dear on the bench through all those cases in which the prosecutors had been called on to disclose particulars of charges in the indictment. She looked at me with all the eager interest of a vicar's wife hearing her husband repeat a sermon she has heard twenty times before, and then, as I sank wearily into my seat, rewarded me by giving a huge sigh and turning to prosecution counsel, saying, 'I needn't trouble you, Mr Plaistow.'

At this the QC, MP subsided gracefully into his seat and Floribel Templett announced her decision. 'It's well known that the government cannot disclose this information to the appellant or his legal advisers. To do so would be to disclose the sources of the information. Mr Rumpole, as is well known, has practised in criminal courts for many years and it appears from his present submission that he is living in the past. It is for us, the members of this commission, to deal with present circumstances and present dangers. No further "details of charges", as Mr Rumpole calls them, will be given to the appellant Khan.'

At this Peter Plaistow climbed to his feet and, smiling obsequiously, said, 'I'm grateful to Your Ladyship.' It was not a pretty sight.

So the so-called appeal of Dr Mahmood Khan carried on with all the good sense of a treasure hunt in a dark room from which the treasure had been carefully removed.

Making what she described as 'a concession to Mr Rumpole's case', Mrs Justice Templett allowed me to call a character witness and Barry Whiteside gave Dr Khan full marks for his honesty, hard work, kindness and decency, and said he found it impossible to believe that the doctor could have had anything to do with any sort of terrorist activity. The judge seemed to take a full note of this and I thanked Barry for his time after Claude had asked a few obvious and ineffective questions such as, 'Can you swear that Dr Khan wasn't meeting terrorists during the hours when he was away from the hospital?', to which the good Barrington could only shake his head and repeat that such conduct would be incredible in the Mahmood Khan he knew and respected. Then the witness left the court after a quick smile in our direction.

We next moved further into the so-called legal procedures of the alleged appeals commission. Claude had to make a speech dealing with the facts of the case and Dr Khan's involvement, and I asked that he should speak first so I might discover what the case was all about.

Of course, this was clearly contrary to SIAC's procedures, having too much of a hint of fairness about it. I could make a speech and then I and Dr Khan and Bonny Bernard would have to leave the court in case we discovered what crimes, if any, the doctor was meant to have committed.

'This precious government of ours,' I had reached the climax, the final, as I thought, unanswerable argument of the one speech I was allowed, 'this government, which wouldn't know a constitutional right if it came up and shouted in its ear, has told us that the terrorists want to destroy our way of life, our civilization, everything we hold most dear.

'Well, all I can say is that our government is working night and day to collaborate with the terrorists. To help them to destroy our civilization and give away our most precious liberties.

'The terrorists would take away our right to juries and give us imprisonment without trial. "You can have it," says the government today. "You can have Magna Carta, we've got no use for it. And while we're about it, we'll throw in the presumption of innocence and the Bill of Rights."

'All I can ask Your Ladyship to do is to reject the illegal instructions of this lawless government and decide Dr Khan's case according to the principles of a fair trial, which we have fought and struggled for over the centuries. Let Dr Khan be told the charges he faces and then let him answer them.'

'Mr Rumpole, have you anything more to say?' Her Ladyship asked me.

'Only this. Ask yourself what justice really means and then do it.'

With this, I wrapped my gown about me and sat down.

'A fine speech, Mr Rumpole.' My client, who had nothing to thank me for, seemed curiously unperturbed by the result of our appeal. I was grateful for his praise;

however, I was less grateful to my instructing solicitor, Bonny Bernard, who put the situation with brutal simplicity.

'Mr Rumpole always makes fine speeches,' he said. 'But, as I'm sure you understand, we lost the case.'

'There's no justice.' Dr Khan shrugged his shoulders.

'Very little of it nowadays,' I agreed. 'But one has to think of another way out. Don't give up hope.'

'I shall not hope.' Dr Khan was still smiling his totally unjustified smile. 'I shall not trust in hope. You will tell my wife all that has happened?'

Bonny Bernard promised to tell her, then Dr Khan returned to Belmarsh and I headed back to Froxbury Mansions with another defeat to notch up on my braces.

12

Extract from Hilda Rumpole's Memoirs

Rumpole came home with his tail between his legs. From the way he behaved, the unusual silence and the fact that he had at least three glasses too many of the wine he brings back from that awful little wine bar, which he seems to prefer to here, I could tell he'd had a bad day. I did my best to cheer him up. In fact I told him that he had performed a public service by keeping at least one more terrorist under lock and key. I said Mr Blair and his whole government, including that Chief Superintendent of Police, who we all respect, would be very grateful to Rumpole for managing not to lose another terrorist in London. I'm afraid telling Rumpole all this failed to cheer him up at all. He's in a difficult mood and I'm sure I'll have trouble getting him to take his Omni Vite in the morning. Well, if he's determined to die I'll have to tell him it's entirely his own affair. I can't take any further responsibility for him.

Rumpole certainly wasn't in the mood to listen to the interesting news I had got from a charming person I met via my bridge club. It all started when Marcia Hopnew (Mash we called her at school) took the odd class 'just to polish up her game'. Mash and I were both monitors in our last year and although she was much cleverer than I was we seemed to hit it off, and I was sorry when we left school and parted. So I was glad enough to see her at the bridge club. I'm making a note here to tell Dodo Mackintosh about this because, at school, Dodo acquired an unreasonable hatred for Mash, who she called a 'stuck-up pig with bushy eyebrows', a description which was 100 per cent unfair.

Anyway, to get to the point, Mash very kindly asked me to play an afternoon's bridge with her husband, who has an important job in insurance and is sometimes able to 'work from home', and a good friend of theirs who had a rare day off from his 'exhausting' job.

So we all met at Mash's delightful mews house just off Lowndes Square and I was introduced to a perfectly charming fellow with grey hair and red cheeks, who smiled at me and said, 'Delighted to meet you, Mrs Rumpole. Of course, I know your husband well.'

Just as I was thinking that there's no one but me who knows Rumpole really well, I mean someone who doesn't just watch him showing off in court but is prepared to look after him twenty-four hours a day, Mash astonished me by saying, 'This is Leonard Bullingham. He's lucky to get a day off from the Old Bailey.'

'The Mad Bull!' How many times has Rumpole come home complaining of the way he alleged this Leonard Bullingham, who was now smiling at me in the friendliest possible way, had treated him in court? And now here was the same 'Mad Bull', sitting opposite me at Mash's lunch table.

We had a really nice quiche with salad and an individual crème caramel for afters. Mash's husband poured a little wine and Leonard (he asked me to call him Leonard) said the judges at the Old Bailey usually took a glass or two at lunchtime. 'Difficult to face your husband, Mrs Rumpole,' Leonard told me, 'without at least a glass of wine at lunchtime.'

'Do you find Hilda's husband so difficult to face?' Mash was interested to know.

'He can be a bit alarming. Intolerant of judges, that's what I'd say about your husband, Mrs Rumpole. Of course, it's all part of the job, I suppose, but I always feel a bit nervous when I've got Rumpole in front of me. I know I've got to keep my wits about me.'

When we cut for partners this Leonard Bullingham and I played together. We didn't exactly win, but we played one memorable hand of four spades. I was dummy and particularly admired the cunning way Leonard finessed the queen.

As I am writing this in the boxroom I can hear the front door and Rumpole's footsteps. They don't sound like the footsteps of a man in a particularly good mood.

Should I tell Rumpole that Leonard Bullingham, as I know him, or the 'Mad Bull', as Rumpole calls him, is quite nervous when Rumpole appears before him? I don't think so. The news would only make Rumpole unbearably pleased with himself, and I'm in no mood for that at the moment.

Oh, and I forgot to say that Mash promised to arrange another bridge afternoon in three weeks' time. Leonard hopes to join us if his present defendant in a long-term fraud pleads guilty.

13

I have to warn anyone thinking of taking up the wig and gown that being a barrister is not half as much fun as it used to be.

The new bureaucracy took a long look at the free and independent life of the courtroom advocate and decided that here was a class of individuals far too free of trivial rules and penny-pinching regulations. So to begin with we each have to acquire a 'practising certificate' at a steep price, which leaves me with far too little to invest in Pommeroy's Wine Bar, or most of Hilda's exorbitant expenditure on Vim and other articles devoted to household cleaning. Speaking for myself, I don't need to practise. Barristers at the level of Claude Erskine-Brown should, perhaps, be allowed to practise at home, but I can do my job perfectly well without this now compulsory control-freakery, having over the years perfected my courtroom technique.

We are now required to fill in forms justifying every minute we spend on a case. Of course, I put in a bill for lying in a bath contemplating my final speech, to which I added the price of heating the water. I also charged for a bottle of Château Thames Embankment, during the leisurely consumption of which I had thought of a new and devastating line of cross-examination. Neither of these claims was met.

Worst of all, we are required to take lessons. I have learned my lessons in a long series of cases, from the interesting moment when I managed to win the Penge Bungalow Murders case alone and without a leader. I can find a fatal flaw in the prosecution case. I can stand up on my hind legs and appeal to the hearts and minds of twelve honest citizens. Such talents require no information technology or mechanical aids. They can only be gained from experience and, only occasionally, listening to even older Old Bailey hacks. I have absolutely no need of classes.

But the rules of the game are that you have to score twelve points a year to stay on as a hack in the Courts of Law, and each class you attend scores you so many points in this radical new game. At first I thought to simplify the process by sending in the sort of little notes children take to school to be excused prep. 'Mr Rumpole is occupied with a double murder and unable to come to school today', or 'Mr Rumpole's cold has gone to his chest and he is hovering between life and death, so may he be excused from this class?' Such words fell into a deep pool of silence, until one day Soapy Sam Ballard, our so-called Head of Chambers, approached my room looking extremely solemn and said, 'This is a serious matter, Rumpole.'

'What's happened now? Has someone been fiddling the coffee money? Or stolen the missing nailbrush in the upstairs loo?' I mentioned the scandals which had previously rocked our chambers to their foundations.

'Worse than that, Rumpole. I have received a serious complaint from the Bar Council.'

'What've you been up to, Ballard – selling T-shirts with "Brief Sexy Sam Ballard for Best Legal Results" written all over them?' Not much of a joke, I'm afraid, but I couldn't resist it.

'The complaint is not about me. It's about you, Rumpole.' He looked as grave as though sentence of death had been passed against me, and he added, 'As I say, it's a serious matter.'

'I don't think we should take the Bar Council *too* seriously.'

'In this case we have to. It seems, Rumpole, that you've been missing classes.'

'They seem to me rather good things to miss.'

'You're wrong about that, Rumpole. You've got to keep up with the times. People have noticed that you're living too much in the past. What's that old case of yours you're always talking about? The Croydon killer, was it?'

'The Penge Bungalow Murders. Have you no sense of history, Ballard?'

'Whatever it was, it's a long time ago. Learn to move with the times. You'd better get yourself off to class, Rumpole. Or they'll take away your practising certificate. It'll be Rumpole out of the Old Bailey.' Here Ballard gave a small wintry smile, as though, in fact, he rather relished the idea.

So I went, like Shakespeare's boy, creeping like a snail, unwillingly to school to learn.

This important change in our legal system, as I had tried to explain to Mrs Justice Templett, meant that our lords and masters had just given away Magna Carta and the Bill of Rights for a pound of tea. These disastrous alterations in the law didn't appear to interest the eager lecturer, a certain Whitlow-Smith, whom I vaguely remembered as someone who made a rather poor fist of a prosecution for dangerous driving at Old Street Magistrates' Court. He had an urgent delivery, which resulted in his words popping out so fast they occasionally obliterated each other. The title of his hour that afternoon was 'Whither Contract?' And our teacher was explaining some sensational developments in the law governing Bills of Exchange when I found myself falling into a light doze.

I was woken by a voice which sounded vaguely familiar. 'My dear, never too old to learn, are you?' I looked up and found myself in the presence of Peter Plaistow, QC, MP. 'I called in at your chambers and they said I'd find you here. I was going to suggest a spot of lunch.'

The life of an Old Bailey hack is full of surprises. There was I, suffering from a lecture on 'Whither Contract?', when I was whisked away for lunch by a QC, MP known to be close to the Prime Minister and constantly to be found strolling up and down the corridors of power. Moreover, when I suggested a pint of Guinness and a steak pie at a pub in Fleet Street, he insisted on taking me to the Myrtle restaurant in Covent Garden – a classy eatery which I hadn't visited since I took Hilda there on our wedding anniversary to discuss the terms and conditions of peace after a fairly chilly east wind had been blowing between us.

The Myrtle was just as I remembered it – full of the faces of celebrities to whom I couldn't put a name, familiar from the pages of Hilda's tabloids. I remembered the snowy-white tablecloths, the waiters wearing white aprons, the low, contented murmur of successful people, accentuated by the popping of corks and the rattle of champagne bottles in ice buckets.

'I've chosen a rather unpretentious little St Emilion, Rumpole. I think you might find it amusing.'

'I'm sure I'll find it hilarious.'

After this Plaistow kept up a more or less sprightly conversation and it wasn't until we reached a longish pause between the potted shrimps and the entrecôte that I discovered the motive behind all this lavish hospitality.

'There's a rumour going round the Temple, Rumpole, that you're writing your memoirs.'

'I have to admit that I will be committing to paper some of the highlights and triumphs, as well as a considerable number of low moments, since I burst upon the legal world, at a fairly young age, as the young white wig who managed to win the Penge Bungalow Murders alone and without a leader.'

'When you publish your memoirs, Rumpole, I'm sure they'll create . . . well, a good deal of interest.'

'Publish them? I hadn't really thought about that.'

'I'm sure you have. I'm sure you know that you've become a bit of a legend in your own lifetime.'

'Do you really think so?'

I was beginning to find his conversation quite agreeable and decided that Peter Plaistow didn't deserve the abuse he got from Hilda's tabloid for being, so they said, the arch sucker-up to the Prime Minister. I accordingly took a generous swig of the wine, which was also extremely pleasant and entirely without jokes.

'It wouldn't be going too far to say,' he said after the steak had appeared before us and he was halfway through his first chew, 'that you are, in legal circles, well on the way to becoming a national treasure.'

This, I felt, was going a bit far. Was Plaistow in some sort of trouble? Was he after a loan from an improbable source? Was he looking for a substantial contribution to the Labour Party? Would I be landed with the bill?

'I wouldn't say that,' I told him cautiously.

'Oh, I would. I definitely would. And by the way, I've got good news about your client Dr Khan.'

'Have you indeed?' I was prepared not to believe it.

'The Court of Human Rights has come out against us detaining suspects in Belmarsh. He's been set free.'

'That's entirely satisfactory.' I celebrated with a generous gulp of the wine. 'I'm glad to hear it.'

'I thought you would be. And in return for that I . . . well, we have a favour to ask you.'

'What's that?'

'My new job in government will be agreed very soon, so of course I have an interest. We don't need a lawyer of your age and stature, one well known for his great performances at the criminal bar, to rock the boat.'

There was a pause while we both ate, then I had to ask, 'Which boat is that exactly?'

'The ship of state, Rumpole. The Prime Minister is doing his best. He's fighting the battle against terrorism night and day. He can't fight with his hands tied behind his back. He can't be handicapped by medieval laws.'

'Magna Carta. The Bill of Rights. You call these medieval laws?'

'I heard what you said in the SIAC hearing.' Peter was still smiling. 'It was a great blessing it was held in private. But if a lawyer of your standing, Rumpole, one who is, as they say, a national treasure, were to go on attacking us in public, well, as I say, it wouldn't be helpful.'

'Why exactly should I want to be helpful to your government?' I was genuinely puzzled.

'I'll tell you why,' Plaistow smiled. 'I'm soon to become the Minister of Justice.'

'I suppose I ought to congratulate you.'

'No need. But I thought I'd give you a good reason for helping me and the PM in the great struggle. I can't speak in terms of a High Court judge . . .'

'I imagine not.' His point was not yet altogether clear.

'But you're working very hard, Rumpole. Too hard for your age.'

'Unfortunately, I'm not. Briefs are a little thin on the ground.'

'Then what about a job with some security? The pace of the bench after the rough and tumble of the bar. Now, the life of a circuit judge . . .'

'Circus judge is what I call them.'

'I've heard you do that. But consider the security, Rumpole. A few years and then a reasonable pension. Of course, it would be quite inappropriate for you to make political statements. How does 'His Honour Judge Rumpole' sound to you?'

I consumed the last of my steak and then I let him have it.

'To me,' I said, 'it sounds disgusting.'

My answer seemed to surprise him and then he said, 'I'm disappointed in you, Rumpole.'

'Not half as disappointed,' I told him, 'as I am with your precious Prime Minister. I shall continue to document the law-breaking conduct of your government. If necessary, from the rooftops.'

'If that's the way you feel . . .'

'It certainly is.'

'Then I'm afraid I can't do much to help either you or your client.'

'Don't worry,' I said. 'We'll do our best to take advantage of the little amount of law still left to us.'

After that conversation began to flow like cement. Plaistow suddenly remembered he had an urgent appointment at the Home Office, so I had to go without pudding. I was relieved to see that he signed the bill before he left me and I saw him winding his way between the tables, shaking some hands and kissing some cheeks by way of greeting his many friends, of whom I was certainly no longer one.

Further embarrassment was spared by the head waiter telling me of a telephone message received from my clerk Henry. An urgent conference in the case of Khan. The clients would be waiting for me on my return to chambers.

14

I started to walk back to my chambers (my present bleak financial situation made it unwise to indulge in a taxi) with feelings of considerable indignation. Everyone, they say, has his price and there just might be some huge bribe or gigantic offer which could delicately be mentioned in conversation with the intention of corrupting Rumpole. But a circus judgeship! To offer me such a bribe as that for betraying my dedication to the basic principles of our legal system was an insult, even in the world of political chicanery. In fact, it showed how inept the government was, even in its most dishonest behaviour. Did they imagine that I, Rumpole of the Bailey, would forsake Magna Carta for the pleasure of sitting in some stuffy suburban courtroom, trying petty crimes and disputes about . . .

Such were my thoughts as I walked through Covent Garden. Then I remembered the days when this was the fruit and vegetable market where farmers set out their produce, where the pubs were open at five o'clock in the morning and barrow boys shouted about their wares and the pavements were littered with discarded boxes and cabbage leaves. Regrettably, it had been tidied up, the market moved to a distant part of London.

I emerged into the traffic of the Strand and then turned into the Temple, under the archway where the newsagent used, in days gone by, to offer the occasional pornographic magazine to solitary barristers. Inside the arch all was quiet. The buildings no doubt contained rooms where tales of vicious murder, fraud and matrimonial infidelities were being discussed, but those doors were kept closed and the courtyards were silent.

When I looked into my chambers room, Henry said, 'At last you're back.'

'I was discussing matters of high political importance.' This failed to impress Henry, who said, 'There's four of them been waiting in your room. Mr Bernard with Mrs Khan and Mr and Mrs Barrington Whiteside. I offered them coffee, which was declined.'

'Thank you, Henry. You did very well.'

I had expected the conference in the case of Khan to be an occasion of rejoicing. For whatever obscure political reason, Plaistow had told me that the good doctor was out of prison, and I expected some totally undeserved but nevertheless pleasing congratulations on the result. I wouldn't have been surprised if the location of the meeting hadn't moved, once again, to Pommeroy's Wine Bar, where the doctor's friend Barrington Whiteside might have placed an order for champagne.

Nothing of the sort occurred. The faces that greeted me in my chambers room were far from joyful. Bonny Bernard looked unusually grim. Tiffany had actually been weeping and her hand clutched a little ball of wet handkerchief. Barrington Whiteside was frowning furiously. Only his wife, Benazir, seemed calm and, I thought, detached from the proceedings. She was a woman in perhaps her fifties. Unlike Dr Khan, she hadn't surrendered to the civilization of Kilburn and the north London suburbs: she wore a bright sari, which was at that moment the only cheerful thing in the room.

'Well,' I said, trying to sound cheerful, 'bit of good luck at last. Dr Khan has been sent home from Belmarsh.'

Bernard made it clear that it was not altogether good news. 'He's under house arrest.'

'It's an outrage,' Barrington Whiteside exploded. 'A complete outrage.'

'He can have visitors,' Tiffany explained. 'He can't leave the house, of course, and I think they are always watching him, the constant telephone calls we receive. He is unemployed now. He's a good doctor and he can't do the work he loves. He can't earn a living for us all. They have cut him off from everything.'

'I'm trying to get my board to agree to go on paying his salary,' Barrington told me. 'But it's going to be difficult.'

'I've written to the Home Office, of course.' Bernard was defensive. '*We've* done all we can. Of course they won't tell us anything.'

'It seems your country is as bad as ours.' Benazir Whiteside spoke for the first time. 'They lock you up and don't tell you why.'

'It's not always as bad as that.' I did my best to defend our legal system. 'We still have jury trials where the prosecution has to present its case. We've got to get that sort of trial for Dr Khan.'

'It's all we're asking for,' Barrington said. 'A trial by jury. Of course they'll acquit him.'

'Get him a fair trial, Mr Rumpole,' Tiffany was pleading.

'We've come for your advice.' The usually helpful Bernard put his finger on the weakness of my attempt to clear up the proceedings. 'How do we persuade the authorities to charge him with some criminal offence?'

'I don't know yet, but I'm going to find a way.'

I looked round at their faces. Had I made them a promise I couldn't keep? Might it not, after all, be preferable to retire quietly from the scene and reappear as a circus judge? They had come to me for help and I had been afraid to admit that the situation was hopeless.

15

Extract from Hilda Rumpole's Memoirs

I really don't know which is worse, Rumpole cock-a-hoop after getting some highly dubious character found not guilty or Rumpole in a dark and melancholy mood after he's lost a case. I suppose cock-a-hoop is better because, although it's a bit annoying when he tells me how cleverly he did it, he's probably quite busy and I don't have him round the mansion flat with nothing particular to do but smoke too many small cigars and make it more difficult for me to lock myself into the boxroom to get on with my memoirs.

He's at a pretty low ebb at the moment because he says he lost the terrorist case. I tell him it's no loss at all. The dangerous doctor (he must be dangerous or the government wouldn't have arrested him in the first place) has been let out of prison on the condition he stays at home, home being, according to Rumpole, an extremely comfortable and roomy house 'at the better end of Kilburn'. This seems to me to be very generous of the government under the circumstances, and I asked if the terrorist's wife, that pool-eyed person Rumpole is always going on about, was confined to their house too.

Apparently not. Apparently she's free to come to Rumpole's chambers whenever she wants, crying her eyes out. I suppose if I had Rumpole in here all day and all night, unable to leave Froxbury Mansions, I might cry my eyes out too but there it is. I tell Rumpole that it's all over now and there's really nothing more he can do about it, but he doesn't seem to be able to put the case behind him and cheer up.

Another annoying thing. Rumpole told me that he was offered 'a circus judgeship'. The offer came through a QC called Peter Plaistow, who is apparently very close to the Prime Minister and who comes across so well when he talks about politics on television. Well, a circuit judge may not be the grandest job in the land. Rumpole would only get to be called 'Your Honour' and not 'My Lord', like a High Court judge. But in my opinion Rumpole ought to be quite flattered to be called 'Your Honour', and it would provide him with a safe job and a pension for us when he retired. 'Why not take it,' I put to him quite tactfully, 'and spare yourself all this anxiety about losing or winning cases?'

'I don't want to do it,' he said. And when I asked him why ever not, he said, 'I might develop "judgeitis".'

Of course, I asked him what that was.

'A ridiculous inflation of self-importance, with increased intolerance; a fatal tendency to suck up to juries, to interfere with the cross-examinations by defending counsel; and doing your best to find all the customers in the dock guilty.'

'That's nonsense, Rumpole,' I told him. 'Leonard's a judge at the Old Bailey and he's not a bit like that.'

'Leonard who?'

'Leonard Bullingham. I met him playing bridge with Mash. He was perfectly charming.'

'You're talking about Judge Bullingham? The Mad Bull?' Rumpole apparently couldn't believe his ears.

'He didn't seem at all mad. He said he enjoyed having you before him, Rumpole. He said he gave you a run for your money.'

'He said that?'

'So far as I remember.'

'Judgeitis.' Rumpole seemed sure of it.

'He sounded perfectly sane to me. In fact, he didn't seem to be suffering from any sort of disease.'

'That's the terrible thing about judgeitis,' Rumpole told me. 'The sufferers don't know that there's anything wrong with them!'

Quite often I really can't understand what Rumpole's talking about. But I will say one thing for him. He's been much better at taking his Omni Vite. It seems, in some ways, as though the fight's gone out of him. At the end of the conversation about Judge Bullingham he actually thanked me.

'You mean thanks for telling you he enjoyed having you appear before him?'

'No,' he said. 'Thank you for telling me his name's Leonard. We always thought he was a Ronnie.'

'Leonard is his second name,' I told him firmly. 'And he definitely prefers it.'

16

There followed a bleak period in the Rumpole career. Not since the early days, when I had sat in what was then Hilda's daddy's chambers, had I faced such an alarming absence of paid employment. I arrived at chambers each day and did *The Times* crossword too quickly. Then I carried on with my memoirs until it was time for the shot of pie and Guinness in the pub, which I began to wonder if I could still afford. Back in chambers I had the first small cigar and fell into a light doze. At around teatime I would go into the clerk's room and ask Henry if I had anything 'in the list for tomorrow'.

'No, Mr Rumpole. You're in luck's way – they're giving you a holiday tomorrow.' This was said, I suppose, in a vain and hopeless attempt to cheer me up. The most encouraging call I had during that doleful period was from Bonny Bernard, who offered to buy me a drink at Pommeroy's that evening at six o'clock. The time-honoured tradition of the drinks at Pommeroy's was that they were marked down on my slate and my most loyal solicitor didn't even bother to look as though he was fumbling for the cash. That he was undertaking to foot the bill raised my hopes of there being a big money brief somewhere in the offing.

These hopes increased as Bonny Bernard handed over

the cash for a bottle of Château Thames Embankment. I complimented him on his generosity.

'That's quite all right. I felt sorry for you after that last conference in Khan.'

'Really? Why?'

'You didn't know what to do next, did you?'

It was an awkward question and I quite failed to give my friend the solicitor a satisfactory answer. 'After Mrs Barrington Whiteside told me to fight on . . . Well, I didn't feel like arguing with her at that particular moment.'

'She's a remarkable woman,' Bernard had to admit. 'She wants to go on fighting and she's paying for it.'

'Really? Is she rich?'

'Her father was. He came from Pakistan, just like the Khans. Apparently he did well in business and left Benazir a packet of money.'

'A rich woman married to the hospital administrator. How did they meet?'

Bereft of a new idea I wanted to spend the time getting to know as much as possible about the enigmatic doctor and his friends.

'Tiffany told me Benazir was always very nice to her after both fathers died. She said the fathers had been friends and she vowed to keep up the friendship. She'd come to the house in Kilburn and say what a lovely house it was, and baby-sit for them. All that sort of thing.'

'And Barrington Whiteside?'

'It seems the Khans invited Benazir to some sort of charity do at the hospital. A dance – that's what I think it was. She met Barry and they fell for each other. Got married within a month or two, Tiffany told me.'

'So with a rich wife – Barrington carried on his hospital job?'

'That's entirely to his credit, wouldn't you agree?'

'Oh yes. Entirely to his credit.'

'They're a caring couple.' The word 'caring', I thought, was an expression used by Mrs Bernard, who worried about the environment and helped her husband get off small cigars.

'Of course,' I agreed. 'That's why I felt I had to promise some further activity. But what, exactly?'

'If you could persuade the Home Secretary . . .' Bernard had downed another glass of Pommeroy's Very Ordinary and was, I thought, letting his imagination run riot.

'Me? Persuade . . . You know who the Home Secretary is, don't you? The Right Honourable Fred, don't you dare call him Frederick, Sugden. The man who has announced he distrusts all lawyers, including judges. The working-class Fred from the back streets of Bristol who made his way up through Reading University to the top ranks of the Labour Party. The friendly statesman who abolished the hearsay rules and allowed the police to impose fines without the necessity of a trial. The statesman who apparently believes Magna Carta should be banned as an obscene publication. I've got about as much chance of persuading him as I have of becoming Lord High Chancellor of England.'

'You'll think of something.' Bernard received my bleak picture of the person in charge without apparent concern. 'That's what I tell clients. Mr Rumpole will think of something.' He drained his glass and added, 'I'm on my way to deliver a brief at your chambers. The Timsons are in trouble again.'

'There's nothing new under the sun. Which one is it this time?'

'He's called Will. I didn't really remember him.'

I remembered him. The Timson who loved Tiffany and hated her husband. All the same, I wasn't about to reject a client.

'I'm glad the Timsons have forgiven me.'

The little flicker of hope which had warmed me when my instructing solicitor mentioned the Timsons died out when he said, 'Oh no. I'm afraid they haven't forgiven you. I'm delivering the brief to Mr Claude Erskine-Brown.'

17

'Now are you going to give up trying to get that ghastly little Dr Khan out of trouble?'

'Not quite yet, Hilda. I don't think quite yet.'

'Well, you're not actually *doing* anything for him, are you, Rumpole?'

'I promised to think of a way of getting him out of his house. I haven't given up yet.'

Hilda was contemptuous. 'I'm sure there are people who got killed or wounded on the tube who would have been glad to settle for house arrest.'

Of course She Who Must was absolutely right. That terrible summer suicide bombers had invaded the Underground, killing innocent, harmless and no doubt decent people. I had been in London during the Blitz, when bombs fell nightly and, in the morning, you found your way past the skeletons of houses along pavements littered with broken glass, but now we had meaningless deaths under a peaceful sky.

I had defended murderers of course, plenty of them from time to time, but at least they had some ascertainable reason for their behaviour. None of them killed total strangers in some idiotic hope of changing the world. And if it were true, if the quietly spoken, smiling, cricket-loving, beef-eating doctor played even a small part in such horrors, he should be locked away for a very long time indeed.

'You do see my point, don't you, Rumpole?'

'Yes, Hilda. I see your point.' There was a minute's silence and then She Who Must looked at me in an amazed sort of way.

'You're not arguing with me, Rumpole.' Hilda was clearly surprised. 'Are you feeling entirely well?'

The situation in chambers at that time was still not conducive to a feeling of well-being and the joy of living. I had rarely seen a mantelpiece so clear of briefs as mine was at that dark moment of the Rumpole career. I had Henry's regular cheerful evening song of 'We're giving you a day's holiday tomorrow, Mr Rumpole' constantly repeated. I was aching to get my teeth into some new legal problem, preferably one unconnected with terrorism. I remembered what I used to do when I was a young and frequently unemployed white wig and before the Penge Bungalow Murders lifted me into a better world. I used to go down to the Free Legal Advice Centre in the East End of London to avoid breaking into loud curses and a furious denunciation of the world of today. It allowed me to remain decidedly calm.

I had kept the telephone number and rang it, in the unreasonable hope of finding Miss Brotherton still in charge. She was a dedicated, overweight young woman who gave us cups of tea and home-made cake and was anxiously polite to anyone accused of a serious crime and impatient with those who only came in to complain about their rent or their child-maintenance support. Instead I got the high-pitched tones of a youngish man who said, 'FLAC here. Sidney speaking. How can I help?'

'Is Miss Brotherton there?'

'I'm afraid I don't know any Miss Brotherton. I'm in charge. Let's have your name.'

'Rumpole,' I said, expecting an immediate change of tone, an amazed respect, which was not forthcoming. Instead I got, 'What's your trouble, Mr Rumboe?'

'My name's Rumpole. RUMPOLE.' I spelled it out for him. 'And I'm temporarily out of work.'

'So are a good many people in the Mile End area,' this Sidney said. 'Have you signed on?'

'Signed on what?' I was not following Sidney's drift.

'At the Job Centre.'

'If you have anyone with a remote knowledge of the law with you this evening, Sidney,' I said, 'mention my name. They will tell you that I have become a sort of legend round the Old Bailey and the more important criminal courts. Being in the unusual position of enjoying a temporary lack in paid briefs I'm prepared to come down and give your non-paying customers free legal advice. Am I making myself clear?'

'That's very good of you, Mr Rumpole.' Sidney, it seemed, had at last got the message. 'We could do with a criminal lawyer. Mr Housegood of Lincoln's Inn was going to come, but his clerk phoned to say he was detained by a case in Shropshire.'

'It will come as a surprise to you,' I was able to say, 'that I have never heard of Mr Housegood of Lincoln's Inn, nor have I met anyone of that name round the Old Bailey. As I say, I expect no remuneration for my services of any sort, but I do appreciate a slice of home-made cake with my cup of tea.'

Sidney's answer merely underlined the decline of standards in public life. 'No home-made cake, I'm afraid,' he said. 'We might manage a couple of organic biscuits.'

Before I could escape from chambers, Erskine-Brown entered my room, collapsed into my client's chair, gripped his forehead and gasped, 'You've got to help me, Rumpole.'

'You've fallen in love again?'

'Not that. You've got to tell me how to deal with the Timsons.'

'That would take a lifetime's experience.'

'I haven't got a lifetime. It's coming on after the holidays. It's Will Timson.'

'What've they got him for?'

'Breaking and entering a corner shop off the Edgware Road.'

'That's a bit far from the Timson patch. They're south London villains.'

'He's said to have done the job with a certain James Jacob Molloy . . .'

'That's extraordinary!'

'Why?'

'The Timsons hate the Molloys. They're deadly enemies.'

'They are still. Molloy's grassed. He's giving evidence for the prosecution. And I'm meant to think of some brilliant defence. You know the Timsons, Rumpole. Would you have a glance at the brief and see if you can come up with any ideas?'

'I'll try and find the time,' I promised him. In fact I was curious to discover a new chapter in the long history of the Timson family. 'You could start by learning about the long rivalry. Then you can tell the jury that Molloy made the whole thing up to get his own back on Will Timson. Make a big thing of it.'

'Will the jury believe that?'

'Probably not. But you'll have had a fight. That's what your average Timson needs, a good fight in court.'

'I advised him to plead guilty.'

'Oh, he won't like that. The Timsons are fighters, so go with it. Excuse me, I've got to be off, pressure of work.'

As I moved towards the door, the unfortunate Erskine-Brown removed the hand from his brow and asked, 'Where are you going, Rumpole?'

'Somewhere where a man might come walking in off the street with a smoking gun and I'd get a brief in a sensational murder. It's called FLAC, Free Legal Advice Centre.'

'I say,' Erskine-Brown looked at me with mild surprise, 'has that ever happened to you, Rumpole?'

'No.' I had to tell him the truth. 'Never at all.'

'So what exactly is your trouble?' I asked the pale, sharp-featured woman on the other side of the desk in FLAC that evening. She spoke in a high, exhausted voice, a voice that seemed almost worn out with complaining, and flicked her hands in the air as though she were brushing away imaginary insects.

She said, 'Truancy.'

I had come down to Stepney Green that evening after my conversation with Erskine-Brown and seen various customers. I sat on a hard chair in a small office and listened to a man who complained that strange voices insulted him whenever he visited the public baths, and to many who had banning orders – known with considerable affection by the government as ASBOs – imposed on them to prevent them sleeping in doorways when they had no houses to go to, begging for small change when they had no money or getting drunk, when any money was available, as a relief for life on the streets. Such orders were imposed on them after no trial or appearance in court of any kind. They were plastered on them by the local police, who were relieved of the tiresome duty of providing evidence or presenting a case. From Dr Khan to the poorest sleeper in doorways, our lords and masters have shown their cheerful contempt for the rule of law.

And now I had to deal with Mrs Nesbit, apparently accused of a new offence of truancy.

'What on earth,' I asked her, 'were you truanting from?' I ran through the possibilities in my mind. Russian lessons? The use of the wok? Embroidery? None of these subjects seemed probable, nor their avoidance a criminal offence.

'It's not me. It's my Natalie. My daughter. They call her partially sighted, which means she's half bloody blind, I reckon.'

'That seems to be a fair translation.'

'She can't see the blackboard so she doesn't like school anyway. And the one she's in means there's a long journey to get there, so she stays away. She stays off school, I know she does.'

'She's the truant?'

'That's it. But it's me that gets the summons.' She pulled out a small folded piece of paper and pushed it across the desk. 'The magistrate's fined me £250 just because

Natalie leaves home in good time but doesn't turn up at her school.'

'Did you tell the magistrate that?'

'No, I didn't. I thought it best to stay away.'

'Why did you think that?'

'I thought they'd know. We're a one-parent family on benefit . . . Our Natalie's restricted vision . . .'

'You should have been there to remind them.'

'I could've told them, yes. I could've told them where Natalie goes when she might not be at school.'

'Where exactly?'

'Round the Osgoods'. At home with the Osgood kids and them that never goes to school. I think Betty Osgood gets them children to talk to Natalie just to get me into trouble.'

'Why should she want to do that?'

My client flicked both hands in the air, as though brushing away all reasonable doubt. 'Because she wanted my flat. She always wanted it.'

'Why's that exactly?'

'Outlook. We look out over all the houses. You can see lots of fields and that, a long way away. All the Osgoods can see from theirs is the walls and windows of the next tower. She thinks if I get into trouble I won't be able to pay the rent. Then I'll have to move out. I know Betty. I know a person like that. I know how her mind works.' And then she became still, her hands locked together on the desk in front of her, her high, chattery voice quieter now. 'You're not going to do anything for me, are you?'

'Of course I am going to do something. That's what I'm here for.' I bit into an organic biscuit and thought about what I could do exactly. Then I said, 'The magistrates should never have made their order without seeing you. They didn't know the facts. We'll get them to rescind it and have another trial.'

'Would you speak up for me?'

Would I? I thought as I chewed the organic biscuit. Appear before the Stepney magistrates for no money? Would I? 'Of course I will,' I told her.

She bent forward then and planted a quick, dry kiss on the hand which still held a portion of biscuit. Then she jumped up, said, 'See you in court then,' and left, relying on me and Sidney to make the necessary arrangements.

I travelled home on the tube, which was now free of all murderous incidents. I felt I had learned something from my evening at FLAC, but looking back on it I could no longer remember what it was.

18

Extract from Hilda Rumpole's Memoirs

At home things seem to have sunk to a new low. Rumpole has been reduced to going to some free law advice place in the East End where he went as a young and briefless barrister. He came back and said he rather enjoyed it, it was 'better than sitting at home watching television'. It's all very well for him. It's a great deal harder for me at the bridge club when people say, 'How's your husband? Busy as usual, is he?' Am I meant to say, 'He's been quite busy giving advice down the East End of London for no money'? I just couldn't put up with all those sighs and looks of sympathy. So I said that Rumpole has been on two or three big cases and left it at that. I think he's extremely lucky to have someone to tell fibs for him at the bridge club.

I should record the fact that the charming judge, Leonard Bullingham, has turned up at the bridge club. There'd been an unexpected guilty plea and he had the afternoon off. We got talking over lunch and the conversation turned to marriage. Leonard told me the sad story of his own, which had ended in divorce. He told me that his wife was 'a perfectly nice woman' but she just wouldn't 'join in'. That is to say, she wouldn't come with him to any legal gatherings or City dinners or even the

Christmas party at the Old Bailey, which Leonard told me was 'no end of fun'. It was because of this not joining in that they separated by mutual consent and eventually divorced. Leonard said he misses her very much but, as she wouldn't join in, he felt he had no further choice in the matter.

He was clearly in an emotional state after telling me all this and I'm afraid to say that we outbid considerably and we were well down on points at the end of the afternoon, which Leonard generously settled up for me. Then he laughed a bit and came out with an invitation to 'join in' with him at some of the legal and Old Bailey dos he'd been talking about. It would be an honour, he said, if I would consent to be his guest. Of course, I said I'd love to, which is true, not least because Rumpole is happier 'joining in' with a bottle of claret in Pommeroy's Wine Bar.

With time apparently on his hands, Rumpole has been watching a lot of television. He particularly likes Jenny Turnbull's interviews with people in the news. She's just announced that she'll be interviewing Fred Sugden, the no-nonsense Home Secretary, who certainly doesn't share Rumpole's liking for criminals. Jenny Turnbull is going to interview him next week in the Inner Temple Hall and members of the public can buy tickets to attend. This has had an electrifying effect on Rumpole, who jumped out of his chair and said, 'That's it. I'll get him then.' I just hope Rumpole isn't about to make a complete exhibition of himself on television. Whatever he's planning to do, I certainly shan't be joining in.

19

To my surprise I got a ticket for the Home Secretary's 'Public Question and Answer' in the Inner Temple Hall. When I went to book my ticket in advance, the girl at the desk had it ready. 'Your ticket, Mr Rumpole.' This pleased me, although I didn't understand the full implications at the time. I felt I had lived through a period of neglect and been restored, at least to some sort of notoriety. Jenny Turnbull's *Up to the Minute* television show had picked on me as a likely speaker to join in the debate.

The hall, when the great night came, was a blaze of light. Cameras were being wheeled among us in search of the most advantageous position. The 'controversial' Home Secretary was sitting on a chair, chatting to Jenny Turnbull, the show's good-looking and usually astute presenter. The only possible way to describe the Home Secretary was to say that he was 'square'. This didn't apply to his musical tastes or even the way he dressed – I know nothing of these matters – but with his broad shoulders and hips he seemed to be a comforting figure of four more or less equal sides. His red hair was turning grey and he had a high-bridged and prominent nose which was a gift to caricaturists.

The proceedings started with Jenny asking the Home Secretary what it felt like to be in the Temple, the home of the lawyers and judges he'd been so critical of in his recent speeches. The Right Honourable Fred Sugden didn't miss the opportunity of reminding his audience that he came from the back streets of Bristol (he called it Bristle, being anxious to preserve his local accent). He knew nothing of what he called 'the Temple of Tradition', where judges and the fathers and grandfathers of judges had grown up with a vested interest in keeping the law unchanged and unchangeable. But judges didn't make the laws, said the Right Honourable Fred, politicians like him who had an 8,000 majority at the last election did, and what did that 8,000, and millions of other voters, really want? They wanted to sleep safely in their beds and they weren't a bit interested in our legal theories carefully designed to keep the crook and the terrorist out of trouble.

When Fred Sugden had finished his opening salvo, Jenny Turnbull announced that it was time for questions and I was first on my feet. Adopting a tone that was reasonable but pained, I led off with, 'I have a client who is under house arrest. He's never been tried. He's got no idea of the reason, if any, for his imprisonment. He can't carry on his work as a doctor. Why can't you charge him with terrorist activities or give him a fair and decent trial in front of a jury?'

'You know perfectly well,' Fred Sugden was smiling politely, 'Mr . . .' Here he turned to Jenny for help. She looked at a bit of paper and said, 'Rumpole,' in an ear-piercing whisper. 'Mr Rumpole, I'd been told to expect a contribution from you. I understand you're looked on as a sort of permanent fixture down at the Old Bailey. Been there as long as anyone can remember.'

'Never mind about me and the Old Bailey. When can

my doctor client be given a fair trial, according to the law?'

'I'm sure, Mr Rumpole of the Bailey,' the Sugden smile widened, 'you're anxious to get a nice fat brief out of a jury trial.'

I may sometimes seem to lose my temper in court, there are moments when it's effective to seem angry, but now I fell into a genuine rage. There was no sort of pretence about my fury with the government representative on this occasion.

'It's not a question of a fat brief!' My voice might have rattled the windows and been heard across the car park. 'It's not only that you seem never to have heard of Magna Carta or the Bill of Rights. Now you've convicted poor people, the homeless, those sleeping in doorways, you've convicted them without any sort of trial, fining them when they have no money, and all on the say-so of overworked policemen acting on hearsay evidence. Add this to imprisonment without trial. Aren't you a lawless government?'

There followed a moment's awkward silence until the minister, still smiling, asked me a question.

'Let me ask you this, Mr Rumpole. How do you take notes in court nowadays?'

'I use a pen and my notebook.' I gave him a truthful answer.

'A pen!' The Bristol accent rose to a high pitch of contempt. 'Would that be like . . . a *quill* pen by any chance?'

There were laughs from the audience, but I put him right.

'No. It's a fountain pen.'

'Really. How very professional. So you're not computer-literate?'

'I'm literate. I know very little about computers.'

'That's the trouble with your sort of lawyer, Mr Rumpole. You can't move with the times. Things like jury trials and the presumption of innocence may have been all very well in their day. But times change. History moves on. We need quicker and more reliable results. Modernize, Mr Rumpole. That's what you need to do.'

I was about to set the windows rattling with another protest when Jenny Turnbull said, 'I think you've had a fair old innings, Mr Rumpole. I'm sure there are a lot of other people with questions.'

So I sat silent. Whatever had happened to me, it certainly wasn't cricket.

'That Fred Sugden seems a fairly straightforward sort of fellow. Did you have to be so rude to him, Rumpole?' was Hilda's comment.

Later Bonny Bernard rang up. 'A memorable performance on the telly,' he said, 'but I thought you'd planned to get round the Home Secretary. Weren't you going to charm him into giving Khan a jury trial?'

I went to bed angry with both of them, but angriest with myself for doing my client no good at all. I dreamed that I had to write the rest of my memoirs on a computer and I couldn't get the hang of the instrument at all.

20

Extract from Hilda Rumpole's Memoirs

It's summer at last. We've had some really hot weather, although not much sunshine in Froxbury Mansions, where Rumpole is still a bit under the weather. He says he's suffering from a medical condition known as *absentia labori* or the diminution of briefs and consequent drying up of the legal aid cheques. I think he's also a bit sore about his failure in the debate with the Home Secretary. 'Well, Rumpole,' I've told him, 'you're never going to be a hit on the box. You'll never be a television star.'

This didn't seem to cheer Rumpole up at all. I don't think he had quite realized how old-fashioned he sounds talking about Magna Carta. As I have told him many times, if King John had had to contend with suicide bombers he might never have signed that thing on whatever island it was on the Thames that he did it. Also Rumpole doesn't realize how absurd it is to stick to writing with that old fountain pen of his that often leaks. Of course, still, he doesn't quite realize that I'm using this computer I bought from Dixons which I really love and on which my fingers are dancing as I write. It will come as a shock to Rumpole when he discovers that I've kept this machine for a long time locked away in the boxroom.

I suppose he'll get even more of a shock when he reads these memoirs. There are a lot of things Rumpole doesn't quite understand.

Well, I've been meeting Leonard Bullingham regularly at the bridge club and quite lately he told me the Old Bailey was on holiday and asked me whether I would join him for lunch at his club next Thursday. He said he'd thought of asking me before but had been too shy to suggest a definite date, and he ended up saying, 'Oh, do say yes, Hilda. It would give me such pleasure.' After that I felt it would be mean to decline his invitation, although I didn't tell Rumpole about it. I thought it would be one of the many things that Rumpole didn't quite understand.

So, last Thursday, when Rumpole had gone off to chambers to do not very much at all, I took a tube down to the Sheridan. I know it's a famous club and when I ask Rumpole why he never joined he always says that he's not keen on the idea of watching judges eat lunch, which was possibly what I was going to do. Leonard, he asked me long ago to call him Leonard, was waiting for me by the porter's desk. I thought he looked nervous, far more nervous in fact than I felt, although I was in strange surroundings and he was, well, sort of at his home.

'So good of you to come, Hilda,' he said. I should have mentioned the fact that he'd called me Hilda over the bridge club table for quite a while now, it was only 'Mrs Rumpole' when we first met. 'I can't take you to the bar,' he said, 'because women aren't allowed in there. So shall we go straight in?'

I agreed of course and we went into a big dining room, where men were sitting together at various tables. There were a few men with women guests at the tables along one of the walls.

'Our table's on the left-hand side of the dining room,' Leonard explained. 'That's because I'm with a woman guest. No women allowed at the tables over there.'

'It seems there are a lot of places I'm not allowed to go,' I told him.

'I just thought I'd explain the club rules to you, Hilda. I take you to be the sort of spirited lady that might protest and insist on being on the right-hand side of the dining room.'

'Don't be afraid,' I said, 'I'm not going to embarrass you.'

'I'm sure you wouldn't, Hilda. And the left side of the dining room's perfectly pleasant, isn't it?'

'Perfectly pleasant.' He was very reassuring, which I found rather touching in a judge.

'I can recommend the roast beef here.' Leonard seemed more relaxed now he'd explained the club rules to me. 'They do a very good Yorkshire pudding here too. And the club claret is excellent.'

'That'll be a change,' I told him, 'from the stuff Rumpole brings home from that dreadful little wine bar of his.'

'What a mistake!' Leonard shook his head. 'Only the best is good enough for Hilda. I have to say, Hilda,' he went on, 'I've been looking forward to this little lunch together for some time.'

'I've been looking forward to it too,' I told him. 'I'm interested in seeing your club from a woman's point of view.'

'That's right, of course. So glad you said that. My wife – well, she's no longer, we're divorced of course

– she didn't visit the club at all. She was a woman who couldn't join in.'

'Well, I don't suppose she could join in at the bar.'

'Oh, that's sharp of you. Very sharp!' Leonard was kind enough to say, and he went on, 'If the day ever comes when they allow women members in this club, which would be over my dead body, you, Hilda, are the first person I'd put up as a female member.'

I didn't ask Leonard how he could put me up as the first female member if the rules had been changed over his dead body. In any event, he clearly meant to be extremely complimentary. However, he was now occupied in placing our order with an elderly waiter who looked at me as though he didn't approve of women in the club, even if we were confined to the left-hand side of the dining room.

'We're having your roast beef,' Leonard was saying, 'and we want a lot of it. I like a lot. And a bottle of the club's excellent St Emilion. Starters? Smoked salmon for starters. You'd agree with that, wouldn't you, Hilda?'

'Yes, of course.' Rumpole hardly ever makes decisions for me. It was a relief to be with a man who did.

We had gone through the roast beef and Leonard had instructed me to choose the profiteroles from the sweet trolley, when he said, 'Rumpole's not an easy man in court. I get the feeling he's not an easy man at home. Would I be right?'

'Quite right,' I agreed with him, my mouth full of profiterole.

'After a divorce, of course, one does get lonely in the evenings . . .'

At this point he was interrupted by a tall, grey-haired

member who stopped at our table and said in a loud voice, 'How are you, Judge? I'll never forget what a good time we had with that buggery in the Euston Super Loo.'

I thought for a long time before writing down that conversation in my memoirs but this is what he really said and Leonard replied, 'Oh yes, that was a fun case, wasn't it? Hitchins, I want you to meet Hilda Rumpole. Rumpole's wife.'

'You're Rumpole's wife?' This Hitchins seemed incredulous.

'Yes, I am.'

'I never thought of Rumpole as *having* a wife. He seems such a one-off. Delighted to meet you, of course. I'd better be making tracks. I'm lunching the chairman of the Law Society.' And Hitchins wandered off to his table on the right-hand side of the dining room.

Leonard finished the last of his profiteroles and leaned back in his chair. 'It's in the evenings,' he repeated, 'that you feel the lack of such a thing as a wife. I can come down to this club, of course. I can share a table with Hitchins, but it's a wife you feel most in need of as the evenings draw in.'

I told Leonard I could understand what he meant and he asked me if I'd ever thought of what he'd been through, that was to say 'divorce'.

'Oh, plenty of times,' I was laughing when I said it. 'You can't live through as many years of Rumpole as I have without thinking of divorce at some of his most irritating moments.'

'Plenty of times!' Leonard looked delighted. 'Well, that's encouraging. All I can say is that Rumpole's a lucky man to have you to come home to, Hilda. And the next time you think of divorce, I'm sure you'll remember this lunch we had together. And now, may I refill your glass with the club's exclusive claret?'

There was no more talk about divorce after that, and following lunch Leonard showed me the club's interesting collection of porcelain and numerous portraits of old judges. Then he put me in a cab (he had an account with this taxi firm). I went straight into the boxroom and added this account of our lunch to my memoirs. I didn't tell Rumpole that I had received what amounted to a proposal of marriage from Judge Bullingham. I didn't mention that fact to Rumpole. I don't think he would quite understand.

In any event, we're off on holiday next week so this is not a time to be rocking the boat.

21

I must say, I have always liked Brighton. It has a slightly raffish air about it, a little tarnished, jovial but not quite respectable, descriptions which have, I regret to say, been applied to Rumpole.

For all the reasons I have gone into so far in these memoirs, we were going through a period of financial restraint, briefs being a little thin on the ground since I had fallen out with the Timson family and, so it was apparently thought among instructing solicitors, failed to shine in my debate with the Home Secretary. All the same, She Who Must insisted that we should, after some years, return to Brighton for a holiday to be chalked up on the overdraft. 'I need to get away from London for a bit to straighten out my thoughts,' Hilda told me, without giving me the slightest hint as to what these thoughts were or why they should need straightening out. So we booked our usual two weeks at the Xanadu and I found myself looking forward to it.

The Xanadu is by no means a stately pleasure dome. It's a small private hotel just behind the seafront on the way to Hove. They did you a perfectly adequate breakfast at the Xanadu and we usually had lunch out, perhaps at a pub somewhere up on the Downs. The sun shone with unusual reliability that summer and we sat in deckchairs reading and listening to the band on the pier.

Hilda insisted we explore the Lanes in search of expensive bric-à-brac. After a bit of hard bargaining she bought a small cut-glass decanter for £20.

'But we've got a decanter,' I reminded her.

'I know we have, Rumpole. But this is a present for a friend.'

'You mean it's for Dodo Mackintosh? I doubt if she'd keep anything in there long. Not judging by the speed at which she downs our sherry.' Her hostility to me and my client, the unfortunate Dr Khan, had left me with no particularly kindly feelings towards Hilda's old schoolfriend.

'No, Rumpole. It's not for Dodo.'

'Well, who then?'

'Oh, just a friend. I do have friends, you know, Rumpole.'

'Yes, of course.' I thought of the numerous old schoolfriends who had visited our spare bedroom in Froxbury Mansions. 'At least,' I said, 'you're not intending to keep that nauseating fluid you used to pressure me to drink in it, are you? It's not for the Omni Vite, is it?'

This was a somewhat challenging remark and I expected a brisk and dismissive reply from She Who Must. In fact Hilda only smiled vaguely and said, 'It's your life, Rumpole, and you must make your own decisions. You lead your life and I'll lead mine. That'll be best, don't you think, from now on.' She was walking along, clutching the wrapped-up decanter in what seemed almost a loving sort of way.

Among the guests at the Xanadu Hotel, the families with well-behaved children, the middle-aged sons with their elderly mother, the two friendly vicars and so on, there was a couple who seemed to take a particular interest in me. He was tall, straight-backed, probably in his fifties, with black hair going grey and clear blue eyes. She looked ten years younger than her partner and talked and laughed a good deal, a plump and cheerful woman who had eyes only for him, but he turned and looked occasionally, and I thought nervously, in my direction.

One morning, Hilda said she wanted to stay in the hotel and write letters. Accordingly I took myself off to the front. I went down the steps to the stony, overcrowded beach and made my way past families and loving, embracing couples, people wriggling into swimsuits behind the cover of towels, others sleeping in deckchairs out of the wind. I crunched my way across the loose pebbles to the edge of the sea.

In my time between Gloucester Road, the Temple and the Old Bailey I thought I lived too far away from the sea, but now there it was, grey and timeless, advancing up the pebbles in a flurry of white foam. I picked up a small, flat stone and tried to send it skimming, bouncing across the water as I had done when I was a boy on holiday, but it was swallowed up by a passing wave and I abandoned the game. I rented a deckchair and sat at the end of a breakwater, watching distant ships on the far horizon, and wondered if I really wanted to go back to putting on a wig to appear before unfriendly judges in stuffy law courts when I could sit in unusual sunshine and contemplate the sea.

After a while, a considerable while, I went up to the pier, which had been almost entirely rebuilt since our last visit. There was still a fortune-teller's booth, which I avoided, having no wish to be told bad news about my future, and a small massage parlour, which I also avoided. Then came a vast amusement arcade. The theatre at the end of the pier had been replaced by a roller-coaster in which screaming people took a sickening journey up and down a railway. I was about to reconcile myself to this sad fact when I saw a poster advertising a theatre in the town where the show sounded promising.

'SEASIDE SENSATIONS,' it read, 'in BRIGHTON for two weeks only with HARRY TURRMAN, a song, a joke and a piano, and the LIDO LOVELIES.' Again I remembered seaside holidays when I was a boy and the shows on the end of the pier, the girls in frilly skirts and pointed pierrot hats with bobbles on them, the whey-faced harlequin who did amazing contortions and the comic who got us all to sing 'Underneath the Arches', my feeling of excitement spiced with terror at the thought of being called up on to the stage.

When I got back to the Xanadu Hotel I found Hilda sitting in the glassed-in veranda, deep in conversation with the plump wife, while the greying husband sat a little apart from them, looking nervously on. Hilda had clearly formed a new and instant friendship with someone she wasn't even at school with, and she introduced me to Myra Antrim and her husband, Ian. It was their first visit to the hotel and Hilda had been giving them tips on the best pubs when walking on the Downs and the cheapest junk shops in the Lanes. When I said I'd got two tickets for the Seaside Sensations show, She Who Must instructed me to get two more so we could have a theatre-going party with the Antrims. This jollification was agreed to in spite of what seemed to me to be the obvious reluctance of Ian Antrim to spend an evening out with the Rumpoles.

Like most things, the seaside show didn't seem quite as good as such shows when I was a boy. There wasn't a white-faced harlequin tying his body into knots, there was no red-nosed comic to make us sing 'Underneath the Arches'. There were constant references to television and the jokes were more slyly sexual than openly vulgar. However, as entertainment it beat sitting in court and losing a case before the mad Judge Bullingham. The first half ended with an energetic song-and-dance number by the Lido Lovelies and then I found myself alone at the bar with Ian Antrim, Hilda having taken Myra off to 'powder their noses'.

As we sipped draught Guinness, Ian looked at me and said, hardly louder than a whisper, 'You won't tell Myra, will you, Mr Rumpole?'

'Tell her what?'

'The Scarlet Band, of course. Myra knows nothing whatever about it.'

'I'm not quite sure what you mean,' I told him.

'We can't talk here. Later, when the girls have gone to bed.' Ian Antrim was looking nervously at our respective wives, who were approaching across the bar, the nose-powdering operation apparently completed. 'All right,' I told him. 'We'll talk later.'

I'm afraid my mind wasn't on the second half of the show. I kept saying 'The Scarlet Band', 'The Scarlet Band' to myself, and then, quite slowly, fragments of memory returned. The title had nothing to do with the Sherlock Holmes story. That was 'The Speckled Band' and it was a snake. This was an organization of would-be revolutionary mates at university. Was it Reading? Perhaps: I couldn't quite remember. Their band was scarlet in the exaggerated way in which the 'Workers' Flag', so the song goes, 'is stained with blood'. They were scarlet, I supposed, because they claimed to be at the reddest, more revolutionary end of Trotskyism, and their occupation seemed to be, when not engaged in lectures or games, protesting.

They found a good deal to protest about at that time – it must have been the late sixties. There was the war in Vietnam, there was apartheid in South Africa, there was the treatment of blacks in the southern states of America and there was Harold Wilson, a British prime minister whom they thought humiliatingly subservient to our transatlantic allies.

To make their feelings felt on all these issues, the Scarlet Band planned a number of outrages on institutions of what they regarded as guilty countries. They didn't attack embassies, these were far too well protected, but they managed to break into a few cultural centres and leave messages of protest and dark threats of sterner measures, including the use of high explosives if the American or South African governments didn't repent. Their activities ended, as I now remembered, when the band set out to attack an American reading room somewhere down the King's Road. They were armed with posters and the threat of 'Arguing the case with bombs'.

The attack was frustrated, however. The police had been warned and before they could reach their objective the band members were arrested. And now I remembered the three Trotskyites who pleaded guilty and for whom

I had the unhappy task of appearing when they were charged with conspiracy to commit criminal damage. With their similar offences taken into consideration, they each got two years and ended their revolutionary lives.

And then, as a long musical number drew to a close, I remembered a tall, nervous figure in the dock, his black curly hair not yet tinged with grey but his eyes even more frightened than they were when he begged me not to say anything to his wife.

It was the end of a long evening. The 'girls', as Ian Antrim called them, had gone to bed. He and I sat in the empty lounge of the Xanadu Hotel, drinking the brandy and soda he'd ordered, perhaps to give himself courage for our conversation.

'I was reading law,' Ian Antrim told me. 'I was going into a solicitor's office. All that had to go because of my conviction. I was lucky I had an uncle in the paint business, so I went into that on the merchandising side, selling paint. It's been a pointless sort of a life really, apart from meeting Myra. She thinks the world of me, Mr Rumpole. She's got no idea I was ever in prison. None of my family told her. Of course I'm happy with Myra, but I can't help looking back on those days with the band. At least we believed in something.'

'I remember my mitigation speech,' I told him. 'I said you were a hopeless bunch of foolish youths who would never have hurt anyone.'

'I know you said that. It made us very angry.'

'If I hadn't said it you might have got three years or four.'

'Perhaps you're right.'

'All those threats of bombing,' I went on, 'did you really mean them?'

'I'm afraid our leader did. One of us had even found a book on how to make explosives in your own back-yard.'

'One of you?' I asked him. 'Which one? Was that you?'

'Not me, no. I mean the one who stayed out of it. The one who never came with us to the American reading room. And I'm sure he was the one who tipped off the police. I suppose he thought it was a better bet to be on their side. We despised him for that, but we didn't give him away. We never referred to him in any of our statements. Well, you may remember that, Mr Rumpole. We never implicated him or anyone else.'

'Who was he then – the one who grassed?'

There was a considerable silence, no sound but the ticking of a clock on the mantelpiece. Then Ian Antrim took a long swig of brandy and soda and gave me the name.

And the empty lounge echoed to the quite unexpected sound of Rumpole's laughter.

I was still chuckling after I'd promised, yet again, not to tell Mrs Antrim or anyone else about my new friend's criminal past. And I was smiling and even uttering an occasional laugh when I turned up in our bedroom and Hilda switched on her bedside lamp.

'What's on earth's the matter, Rumpole?' she said. 'I didn't think any of the jokes tonight were particularly funny.'

'One of them was,' I told her. 'One of them was very funny indeed.'

After that evening at the summer show I was anxious to

get back to my chambers in the Temple in order to make the best possible use of the information I had received from Ian Antrim, but She Who Must would have none of it. 'You've got no work to get back to, Rumpole,' she told me, 'so don't pretend you have. You're not going to spoil Brighton. What you want is a good blow on the Downs and let's hope to send you back in a better state of health than if you were in that stuffy old room in those chambers of yours.'

The Antrims had left the day after our visit to the summer show and my late-night conversation with Ian. When they had gone I was, I'm afraid, a poor companion to Hilda. Too often, on our walks or during pub lunches and evenings in the hotel, she had come out with, 'Rumpole! You're not listening to a word I'm saying,' and too often this was true. All I could think of was a dark cupboard in the corner of my room in chambers, and wonder whether or not I might find something of great importance there.

At last, it seemed at long last, I was released from holiday and we returned to Froxbury Mansions. Early next morning, after a snatched breakfast in the Tastee Bite in Fleet Street, I opened the cupboard in which I kept pile after pile of photographs, copies of letters and odd exhibits from the more memorable cases I'd been engaged in over the years.

The Scarlet Band's plea of guilty was not remarkable, and it was a long time ago, but I had a vague recollection of a photograph which I had kept, for some reason, perhaps as a record of the fervent political years of the late sixties. I'd been searching for an hour or two and had covered the floor with dusty documents when at last I found it. I took it to my desk, switched on a light and examined it carefully and then, I have to admit, I laughed again.

It was a photograph, taken for some underground publication which never used it, but which had, for some reason, been included in my brief at that time. It was captioned 'The Scarlet Band, the group waging war against the enemies of Vietnam'. I could recognize the three youths I had mitigated for when they pleaded guilty, including the young and intense Ian Antrim. But with them was a fourth, another undergraduate, the one who didn't join in the attack on the American reading room, he who thought it a better career move to call the police. Of course, he was younger then, but the square body and naturally pugnacious features were unmistakable. It was the young Frederick Sugden.

22

Having come by such a precious nugget of information about the Home Secretary I was, for a while, at a loss to know what to do with it. I had to confront the elusive Sugden, in some more or less private place, and win his support for the fair and legal trial of Dr Khan. But how to do so? My telephone calls went unanswered. I could hardly shout down at him from the public gallery of the House of Commons or yell after his government limousine in the street.

The answer came with the unlikely presence of Claude Erskine-Brown, who called in to my room for an idle chat which began with a discussion of our recent holidays.

'So you went to Brighton, did you, Rumpole? Lucky you.'

'I think so. And where did you go, Erskine-Brown?'

'St Tropez.' Claude said it dolefully, as though his holiday had consisted of a wet weekend in Wigan.

'That sounds exciting.'

'Exciting!' Claude gave what can only be described as a bitter laugh. 'It was a disaster so far as I was concerned. Peter Plaistow had taken a house there and he invited Philly, so of course she took me and the children.'

'Of course.'

'I thought it would be a good time for all of us. But the other guest . . .'

'What other guest?'

'The Home Secretary. Your friend Fred Sugden.'

'Who said he was my friend?'

'You were on television with him, weren't you? Come to think of it, he stitched you up properly on that occasion.'

'I don't think you'll find that he stitched me up,' I said. 'But go on. What was wrong with him on holiday.'

'Philly took a shine to him. I'm afraid . . .' Here Claude shook his head gloomily. 'It was a distinct shine. You didn't find him attractive, did you, Rumpole?'

'Not my type.'

'She says it's the power. The feeling that he's got power. That's what makes him so attractive.'

'She's not going to leave you for this Sugden, is she?' I had to ask.

'Oh, not that. But she's always having dinner with him. In the Myrtle and such-like places. She went to watch him in a debate in Parliament. I don't think he's at all attractive, but he's got power. We haven't got power, I suppose, have we, Rumpole?'

'I don't know. I might have a bit of it. Does Sugden come to your house occasionally?'

'Our summer party.' Claude nodded unhappily. 'She's asked him and he's coming. She'll flatter him, of course, and he'll ignore me entirely. That's what he did in France.'

'Your wife, Phillida,' I told him, 'in spite of her elevation to the bench, is a very attractive woman.'

'I know that. Of course I know it.'

'Why don't you invite me to your summer party?'

'Well, yes. Yes, of course.' Claude seemed somewhat taken aback. 'What do you have in mind?'

'I might be able to reduce the Sugden power a little. Anyway, Hilda enjoys a party.'

'Reduce his power? How on earth can you do that?'

'I'm not at liberty to tell you how. Not for the moment. But invite us and let's see what I can do.'

The Erskine-Brown house in Islington has a small garden which, for the night of their summer party, was decorated with coloured lights hanging from the trees. House and garden were filled to near-overflowing by judges, barristers, occasional Lords of Appeal – the friends Phillida had made since her elevation to the bench – and the journalists and broadcasters plus the occasional MP who inhabit that part of London. I had glimpsed the Home Secretary often in this throng, usually in close proximity to our hostess, but I had never got near enough to him for a private conversation on a delicate subject.

Then the time came when I saw that Phillida had walked up to the sitting room alone to greet the Lord Chancellor and, looking out of a window, I could see Sugden temporarily on his own, sitting next to an ornate Victorian birdbath, balancing a plate of food on his lap. I hurried down the stairs to join him.

'Good evening, Rumpole. I see you've kept yourself off the television lately.' Sugden was smiling broadly as I sat down beside him. Then he looked distinctly put out. 'You'd better not sit there. I think our hostess will be back in a minute or two.'

'I know she will. That's why we haven't got much time to talk about something rather important.'

'Oh yes? And what might that be?' Sugden was in the act of carrying a forkful of asparagus risotto, with shavings of cheese, to his lips. He returned the forkful uneaten when I said, 'The Scarlet Band.'

'I don't know what you're talking about.'

'I rather think you do. I happen to have a photograph of you in your student days. Taken for an underground magazine. You were clearly in the band.'

'Keep your voice down.' Sugden looked around at the risotto-eating guests, who were clearly taking no interest in him at all.

'You'll remember I appeared for the rest of the band when you grassed on them.'

He looked pleadingly at me and almost whispered, 'Quiet! For God's sake!'

'Oh, it wasn't a serious organization. I mean, you were only amateur terrorists, weren't you? You only trashed a few American and South African properties. I know you talked about bombs. Big bomb talk – and you had the bomber's handbook. I'm not saying you once had a talent for being a terrorist, and you were probably right to adopt the profession of a police informer.'

'Rumpole!' His voice was now hardly a croak. 'What're you going to do with that photograph?'

'Sell it to the papers, of course.' I did my best to sound cheerful. 'I thought I'd start with the *Sunday Fortress*. It's not a sex scandal, but they'd probably come up with a good headline. "Home Secretary was Big Bomber", something along those lines.'

There was a silence between us, and then he asked, 'What do you want?'

'Something quite simple. A fair trial in front of a jury for Dr Mahmood Khan, at present under house arrest. You'll remember the name, won't you? Mahmood Khan, late of Belmarsh Prison. Just a fair trial. That's all he wants.'

'This is blackmail!'

'Exactly. We've all got criminal tendencies, haven't we? I'll give you three weeks – that should be quite enough time to charge him with some offence. If nothing's happened by then – well, read the *Fortress*.'

Before Sugden could reply, Phillida came back and I surrendered her seat to her.

'So glad you came, Rumpole,' she said. 'I hope you and Hilda are enjoying the party.'

'Of course,' I said. 'And congratulations! The party's an enormous success.'

23

'How did you manage it?'

'I made a private application to the Home Secretary. I put it to him in a way he couldn't refuse.'

'An application?' Bonny Bernard had looked puzzled. 'I don't believe I instructed you to do any such thing?'

'No, Bernard, you didn't instruct me. On this occasion I had to act quite informally.'

'I must ask you what you mean by that.'

'I think it's much better if you don't know.'

My application had, in spite of Bonny Bernard's unspoken criticism, had the desired result. Dr Khan had been formally charged under the Terrorism Act with conspiring with others to commit acts of terrorism and failing to inform the police when he knew that such acts were planned.

After these charges had been brought, we had a conference at Dr Khan's then place of arrest, his desirable residence on the sunny side of Kilburn of which everyone spoke so highly. I could see their point: it was a substantial mid-Victorian house with balustraded steps leading to a front door between pillars. The rooms were high and spacious, with long windows giving a view, from the sitting room, of a small, neat garden ending in tall trees. Tiffany, who fluttered nervously round the room, told us that she was the gardener. Her husband sat motionless in an armchair, no longer the neat figure I had seen in prison and when we appeared before SIAC. He looked as though he hadn't shaved that morning, his hair was unbrushed and his feet were half in a pair of bedroom slippers with their backs trodden down.

'Do you think we'll win the case now?' Tiffany asked me as she fluttered. 'Please say we're going to win.'

'I can't guarantee it.' I had to tell the truth. 'Forecasting the result of a case is as dangerous as forecasting the winner of the four-thirty at Cheltenham.'

'If we don't win,' Tiffany came to a halt in front of the marble fireplace, 'quite apart from what'll happen to Mahmood, well, we'd have to sell the house. The hospital's stopped Mahmood's money. We'd have to sell the house to keep me and the children.'

'It was my father's house.' Dr Khan spoke quietly without looking at us. It was as though he was talking to himself. 'He lost so much of his business. All his shops. But he kept the house. For the family. For me and my children. We can't lose it, Mr Rumpole. We can't lose this case.'

I didn't bother to argue, or ask why losing the house would be worse than a four-year stretch as a guest of Her Majesty. I merely said, 'Don't let's talk about losing. We haven't seen the prosecution evidence yet.' And with that I left Dr Khan safe in his house, at least for the time being.

My successful application to the Home Secretary in the case of Khan led to a distinct improvement in the Rumpole practice. Briefs began to reappear on my mantelpiece and Henry, thank goodness, gave me fewer days off.

None of the cases that Bonny Bernard and others sent me were as sensational as that of Dr Khan, but they included Will Timson's bit of trouble. Apparently he had taken unkindly to Claude's often-repeated advice to him to plead guilty and he had decided to break the family embargo and send for Rumpole.

So I found myself conducting my business as usual in the interview room at Brixton Prison, discussing the breaking and entering of premises at numbers 33 and 35 Heckling Street, off the Edgware Road, not a general grocery but a shop selling computers, iPods, DVD players, television sets and other such valuable items. Will's story was, like other Timson stories, not an exactly easy one to put across to a jury; but unlike the rest of the Timsons, he'd become friendly with one of their traditional enemies, a Molloy. Will and Jim Molloy had, he said, 'hit it off', which meant they enjoyed more expensive cars and 'better types of girlfriends' than was usual among the Timson family.

Will said that Jim asked him to join in the robbery, but having inspected the premises by daylight, Will decided against it and he took no part, he said, in breaking and entering the shop by night. However, having taken a number of cheques and loose cash, Jim deposited the rest of the stolen property in Will's garage. When, 'acting on information received', the police questioned Jim Molloy, he told them that Will Timson was the sole thief, an accusation borne out by his possession of the stolen property.

'And you're going to say you didn't know it was stolen property?'

'Of course I didn't.'

'It'll be hard to get a jury to believe you.'

'But you'll do your best for me, won't you, Mr Rumpole?'

'Yes, of course.' I couldn't resist a small sigh at another thankless and probably hopeless task. 'I'll do my best.'

'It was a Paki ran that shop, wasn't it? Another Paki.'

'What's that got to do with it?'

'I'm thinking about that Paki you're defending. The one that took Tiffany away from me. He's guilty as hell, isn't he?'

'Not yet. He's innocent until somebody proves otherwise.'

'I hope they lock him up in that Belmarsh and throw away the key. Traitorous bastard.'

'You know I'm going to do my best for him too,' I told Will Timson.

I thought of Dr Khan, unkempt and untidy, sitting in his carpet slippers, a prisoner in his own home. He had some good friends, hadn't he? And at least one deadly enemy.

24

Extract from Hilda Rumpole's Memoirs

Well, of course Rumpole is cock-a-hoop because his terrorist doctor is going to be tried by a jury and not just kept locked up at home and out of harm's way. Rumpole says it's all due to a 'little chat' he had with the Home Secretary at the Erskine-Browns' very successful summer party. This is hardly likely, as Rumpole was only sitting with Fred Sugden for about ten minutes, so that could scarcely have made a difference. Obviously these things are decided long before and it only goes to show how fair our government is (perhaps far too fair), even to terrorists.

The Erskine-Browns' summer party was a huge success, with so many important legal figures there. I got into a really interesting conversation with the Lord Chancellor, nothing dry and legal, but he was so interesting about the plans he had for building an ornamental bridge over the stream at the bottom of his garden in Surrey. Then he took my plate and stood in the pudding queue for me (delicious lemon tart and crème brûlée). I thought of writing to Dodo to tell her the Lord Chancellor stood in the pudding queue for me, but there is a limit to the amount one should show off, even to Dodo Mackintosh. He said it was an honour to get my pudding because my husband was a legend within the bar. I felt like saying, 'What's the use of being a legend if you can't afford a house in Surrey with an ornamental bridge over the stream?'

But what I need to record is my evening out with Leonard. After our lunch at the Sheridan Club, he invited me to an evening at the 'flicks'. He said there was a flick he wanted to see at his local cinema so what about an evening show and an Indian meal afterwards? Well, it was a tempting offer and Rumpole has been in such a gloom lately, that is before he got cock-a-hoop, that I immediately said yes to Leonard's plan. I told Rumpole I was going out with an old schoolfriend, Patsy O'Neil. In fact I hadn't seen Patsy for yonks but, as usual, I didn't want to stir up trouble by mentioning Leonard's plan.

As I have said before, I don't know what's worse, Rumpole cock-a-hoop or Rumpole in the dumps. When he's cock-a-hoop he bangs round the flat, singing old songs like 'Smoke Gets in Your Eyes' or 'The Man on the Flying Trapeze', which were popular donkey's years ago when he was young and listening to Radio Luxembourg. He also takes over the washing up, using so much soapy water it all has to be done again. When he's in the dumps he just sits around quietly, occasionally saying, 'I think it's time I retired from the bar.' Perhaps, having thought about it, the dumps are better, or at least quieter.

Anyway, I met Leonard at the local cinema in Ealing, where he now lives in what he calls 'solitary splendour'. We sat together in the dark while around us everybody seemed to be eating. Some of them held huge bags of popcorn, others were unwrapping sweets. A man in the row in front of us was apparently pouring what was left of a drink from a thermos flask into a china mug. When the film came on it was a 'romantic comedy' about a couple who were always quarrelling. They had a dog and a child. About halfway through the film the dog disappeared and then the child who went off in search of it disappeared too. After numerous adventures, some comical and others scary, the child and the dog and the parents were all reunited.

As the lights came up in the cinema I saw that Leonard had taken off his spectacles and was wiping what were apparently tears from his eyes.

'Moving, wasn't it?' he said. 'Extremely moving.'

'Well, at least it ended happily.'

'The moment they found the dog! I thought that was very moving indeed.' Leonard blew his nose and put his spectacles back on. 'Now, what do you say to a dish of tandoori chicken, vegetable curry and all the trimmings?'

The Indian restaurant in Ealing was just like an Indian restaurant anywhere else. It had golden-flock wallpaper and a big colour photograph of the Queen, with a couple of brass elephants on each side of the bead curtain that led to the kitchen.

After the tandoori chicken, when we were polishing off some ice cream and the remains of a couple of lagers, Leonard said, 'I have had some extraordinarily good news.'

'I'm glad to hear it.'

'I've had the news but of course I'm not allowed to tell anyone until it's published officially. But if my wife had been here tonight, joining in, I'd've told her on the strict understanding that she didn't spread it around or tell anyone else. If it got spread around, then I might not get it.'

'So you can't tell your wife?'

'My divorced wife? I'd be mad to tell her.'

There was a pause. Leonard took a swig of lager, then he said, 'I think that our friendship is such that we have learned to trust each other.'

'I suppose so.'

'Then in the enforced absence of my wife, I think I shall tell you, Hilda.'

'Please don't.'

'Why ever not?'

'Too much responsibility,' I began to say, but he started telling me regardless.

'This government, and I never thought I'd be able to say this of a Labour government, is turning out to be extremely sensible. The Home Office has no faith in the usual brand of judge material, civil lawyers who know all about libel or slander but turn out to be soft on crime and soft on the causes of crime. They have decided to go where it is well known that the judges are tougher, where we don't let crooks slip through the net by relying on some outdated legal theory. The Old Bailey's a place where we have learned to modernize. So you know where I shall find myself when the announcement is made?'

'Where's that exactly?' I knew he wanted me to ask.

'On the High Court bench – Mr Justice Bullingham – in scarlet and ermine,' and he added what he had said of the Indian dinner, 'and all the trimmings.'

No sooner had he said it than he looked afraid of what he'd done. 'You won't tell anyone, will you?'

'Not a soul,' I tried to reassure him.

'Particularly, you won't tell Rumpole?'

'I won't tell him,' I promised.

'Does Rumpole know we're going out together this evening?' Leonard still seemed distinctly nervous.

'Rumpole,' I assured him, 'has no idea.'

'Just as well,' Leonard said, and drained his lager.

When I got home I found Rumpole reading the papers in some new case he was doing. He seemed cheerful, on the way to cock-a-hoop perhaps, but not yet annoyingly there. He asked me how I'd got on with Patsy O'Neil.

'Oh, fine,' I told him. 'She cried in the cinema when they got reunited with the dog.'

That was all I told him. I didn't tell him Leonard's news because I knew it would put him right down in the dumps.

25

I turned a page of *The Times* newspaper and laughed so hard that I almost spluttered out a mouthful of toast and knocked over my breakfast egg.

'Rumpole! Whatever's the matter?'

'The world's gone mad!'

'That's nothing new, is it? You're always saying it.'

'I know I am, but not quite as mad as this. They've gone and made the Mad Bull a High Court judge.'

'The Mad Bull?'

'Mr Injustice Bullingham. That's what he's become.'

'Oh, I know that.'

I looked at Hilda amazed. 'How on earth did you know?'

'Oh, I think they were talking about it at the bridge club.'

'The Mad Bull must've been shouting his mouth off as usual. Well, well! The Lord Chancellor must've been drunk to appoint him.'

'The Lord Chancellor doesn't get drunk, Rumpole.'

'How do you know?'

'We had quite a long chat at the Erskine-Browns' summer party. He stood in the pudding queue for me. He was absolutely charming and perfectly sober. I'm sure he wasn't drunk when he appointed Leonard Bullingham.'

'All right. If you say so.' It was clear that She Who Must Be Obeyed mixed in legal circles far above me.

*

When I got to chambers there was another bundle of papers on my mantelpiece. These contained the first blast of the prosecution evidence against Dr Khan. He had received and preserved letters which clearly stated that he supported and encouraged terrorism and was aware of a terrorist plot to place bombs in the Tower of London and other national monuments and failed to inform the police.

I lit a small cigar and started to read the translation of the letters apparently found in Dr Khan's possession. If these documents were to be believed, the quiet doctor, Tiffany's beloved husband and the father of her kids, was a brother in the Holy Jihad, who wished to spill as much Jewish and 'Kaffir' blood as possible before he had to appear before his God. Not only were famous buildings to be targeted but wherever people congregated, for instance on New Year's Eve in Trafalgar Square.

Dr Khan was thanked for his financial contributions (cash transactions only) and for his offer to help as a doctor for anyone injured in the Holy War.

Even more chillingly, one of the letters suggested an attack on the Oakwood Hospital, or any part of it which treated Jewish patients. In another letter Dr Khan was thanked for his visit to a 'safe home' when further plans had been discussed. This letter, like most of the others, expressed the hope that the good doctor would, at the end of his life, be able to face Allah with a sufficient amount of blood on his hands.

The letters, and I have only given a brief synopsis of them, were indeed sickening and I felt an unusual surge of loathing for my client, the quiet doctor who watched cricket, respected the Queen and wanted to die with as much innocent blood on his hands as possible. I had won him a fair trial, but thought that once the jury had read half the letters they were clearly sure to convict.

For at least five minutes even my faith in Magna Carta wavered. Was the pugnacious Sugden in fact right? What was so wrong with locking such an offender away in Belmarsh for the safety of the innocent Jews and Kaffirs he was plotting to kill? But then I lit a small cigar and came to my senses. The letters had to be dealt with as though they were run-of-the-mill prosecution evidence in any other case with any other client. I rang Bonny Bernard and told him that we must have an immediate conference to get our client's explanations of these letters found, according to the written evidence of the Special Branch officer, in the desk drawer in his office in the Oakwood Hospital Relatives' and Visitors' Centre. I tried not to betray, by my tone of voice, the fact that I was beginning to hold the same view of our client as that expressed with such certainty by She Who Must Be Obeyed and her old schoolfriend Dodo Mackintosh.

'So we'll have to make another visit to the desirable residence in Kilburn,' I told my instructing solicitor.

'Not much point in that,' he said. 'Dr Khan's no longer there.'

'They set him free?'

'Hardly. He broke the conditions of his house arrest. He made a telephone call, a personal call to someone outside. So the doctor's in the nick.'

'Which nick exactly?'

'Brixton.'

'Along with most of our clients. Make a date, Bonny Bernard, for the usual interview room.'

*

'I know nothing about these letters, Mr Rumpole, sir. I know nothing whatsoever.'

Dr Khan had smartened up again since he left home. He had shaved, his hair was neatly brushed and he looked neat in a prison shirt and trousers.

'These letters,' I reminded him, 'were found in a locked drawer of your desk in the Relatives' and Visitors' Centre at Oakwood Hospital. What do you usually keep in there?'

'Notes about patients.'

'What else?'

'Perhaps letters from ex-patients about their progress. Some letters from GPs. A bit of loose cash sometimes. Perhaps a few private letters.'

'Private letters like these?'

'No, Mr Rumpole. No private letters at all like these.'

'There must be an explanation for the letters. Mr Bernard has seen the originals. Can you tell Dr Khan about them?'

'Special Branch showed them to me. They're all typed in what's apparently Urdu, no envelopes and no dates. There are about ten letters on cheap lined paper. No fingerprints.'

'Produced by a typewriter and rubber gloves. With no handwriting anyone can recognize. But Dr Khan, you must have seen these letters before in your desk. How do you explain them?'

'I told you, Mr Rumpole, I can offer no explanation.' He smiled then, as though once again he found the situation unfortunate but comical. 'I can offer no explanation for most of the things that have happened to me since the morning of my arrest.'

'Do you deny that you know of these terrorist plots to bomb national monuments?'

'Utterly.'

'Or that you gave terrorists money?'

'How could I? Tiffany and the children's school fees take most of my salary. I have a beautiful wife, Mr Rumpole, who likes to dress well. I don't begrudge her any of it, but it doesn't leave us with much.'

'Were you considering an outrage on some Jews and Kaffirs – I take that to mean Christians?'

'I am a doctor, Mr Rumpole. I have sworn the Hippocratic oath – how could I possibly commit murder?'

In the way many doctors have, I thought of saying, from Dr Crippen onwards. I didn't say that, but I felt that I was losing faith in my client. It's not a difficult thing to do. Indeed, with clients like mine faith is difficult to maintain. My own beliefs are of course quite irrelevant. It's for a jury, properly directed, to decide guilt or innocence. If barristers were to decide cases, the whole of our adversarial trial system would grind to a halt. I do my best not to bring my beliefs into court with me. My belief, like my disbelief, is suspended together with my hat and old raincoat in the robing-room cupboard. There is no other way you can function as a criminal defender.

And yet, even if it was breaking the rules, I began to disbelieve Dr Khan. His answers were too pat, his disarming smile too readily available, to carry complete conviction. A doctor might be expected to know the contents of his own desk.

'Did you always keep that drawer locked?' I asked him.

'Yes.'

'And the key?'

'I kept it on my keyring.'

'Where's the keyring?'

'In my house. With my things Tiffany is looking after in Kilburn. I didn't want my unfortunate keyring to follow me into custody.' He gave a little polite laugh, but I didn't join him. Things had gone beyond a joke.

'By the way, and while we're on the subject, who did you telephone? I want to know about the call you made which ended your house arrest.'

'That,' Dr Khan had stopped smiling, 'is a private matter.'

'You've been charged with a most serious offence, Dr Khan. Nothing about you is private any more.'

'I phoned the authorities here. In Brixton Prison.'

'What on earth about?'

'About a prisoner here. He was using his precious phone calls to ring my Tiffany and telling her to leave me. Now everyone knew I was a terrorist, she should "kick me out", he said.'

'And who is this prisoner?' I was afraid I knew the answer.

'A man called Will Timson. On remand also. I know he's always had a thing for Tiffany and he wanted to marry her. But his calls began to annoy her.'

'Have you seen him in here?'

'Not as yet. Perhaps he's on another wing.'

'Just as well. I think you should do your best to avoid his company.'

Of course, I remembered what Will Timson had said to me. He wanted Dr Khan incarcerated for a long, preferably an indefinite, period.

26

Extract from Hilda Rumpole's Memoirs

I had expected, ever since I went to the flicks with Leonard, that my life might get more exciting. The fact is that ever since the piece appeared in *The Times* about Leonard being appointed to the High Court bench and becoming a Red Judge, things have been more than a little slow. I got a rather boring email from Dodo, saying she was 'sketching in the Dordogne'. I don't suppose she gave a thought to the question of whether or not I might have liked a trip to the Dordogne, even considering the number of times that she's had my hospitality here. She says she's met a really fabulous Frenchman who takes their class and does 'watercolours in the manner of Monet'. I bet he's some fat little person in a beret who'll dump Dodo as soon as the trip's over. I've completely decided not to take her into my confidence on the subject of Leonard. She knows nothing, and it's not her business anyway.

I was having lunch all by myself in the kitchen (cheese on toast and a cup of decaff) when the phone rang in the sitting room. When I almost ran to answer it (I really wanted something to *happen* that day) a voice said, 'This is Mr Justice Bullingham's clerk speaking. Is Mr Rumpole at home by any chance?'

'No!' I said. 'Mr Rumpole is not at home.'

Then I heard a voice which I took to be Leonard's saying, 'Ask if he's coming home for lunch.'

'Will Mr Rumpole be home for lunch at all?' the obedient voice took over.

'No, he will not. He's been in Brixton Prison. He'll probably call in at some ghastly pub on the way back to chambers.'

'The lady says he's probably out at some ghastly pub, My Lord,' I heard the voice report. And then Leonard's voice saying, 'Give me the phone, Barnes.' And the newly appointed High Court judge said to me, 'Are you there, Hilda?'

'Yes,' I said. 'And I've been here all along.'

'I just had to make sure that Rumpole wasn't there with you. We're alone. What I have to say is going to be difficult enough anyway.'

'Why is it so difficult?'

'Difficult, and I'll find it extremely painful. By the way, what did Rumpole say when he read of my appointment?'

'I'm afraid he laughed.' I shouldn't have said that, but I was still a bit annoyed at all the mystery.

'Rumpole must have the most extraordinary sense of humour.'

'I'm afraid he has.'

There was a long pause so that I thought he'd gone away and then Leonard spoke in a sort of whisper, I imagined with his mouth very near the phone. 'Hilda,' he said, 'we must face up to the fact that we mustn't meet for a considerable time.'

I was puzzled. At last I said, 'Even at the bridge club?'

'I shall have to avoid the bridge club now for the next . . . well, it may be months. It will be very hard for me to do so, but it's a professional necessity. It's a matter of duty.'

'You mean Red Judges aren't allowed to play bridge?'

'No, it's not that. It's just that I've been selected to try a case Rumpole's in. I think they wanted someone tough who wouldn't stand for any nonsense. It would be quite wrong for me to be seen consorting with his wife, up to and during the trial.'

'Consorting?' I wasn't sure I liked that word. 'Is that what we've been doing?'

'After the verdict of course,' Leonard avoided my question, 'we can do as we like. I look forward immensely to dining with you at the Sheridan. What a wonderfully happy time we had there, didn't we?' And then in a loud voice I heard him say, 'All right, Martin, I'll be with you in a moment.' He explained in a final whisper, 'That's the Master of the Rolls. We're both going across to the Inn for lunch. I'll be thinking of you, Hilda.' And the line went dead.

I didn't know what to think. I went back to the kitchen and did something I rarely do. I poured myself a large glassful of what Rumpole calls his Château Thames Embankment. I thought it tasted rather nice, so I gave myself another glass as I tidied up the kitchen.

27

'The police didn't come and ask you if they could go through Dr Khan's desk? Perhaps when he was away on his holiday around Christmas last year?'

'Nobody came.'

'Nobody with anything so old-fashioned as a search warrant?'

'No one at all. I've talked to the other members of staff. They can't remember anyone asking to go through Mahmood's desk and papers. Of course, no one will have been allowed to search unless they had a warrant.'

'Perhaps Special Branch was doing a little unauthorized breaking and entering. They rather enjoy that.' I was with Bonny Bernard and Barry Whiteside in the Relatives' and Visitors' Centre at Oakwood Hospital. It was a small house at the end of a garden, originally perhaps a dower house set apart from the main building, which had been pulled down when the hospital was built. The front door had an old-fashioned lock, not even a Yale, which was opened by a key which was kept overnight up at the hospital. It was not, however, a lock which would have given much trouble to a policeman or a criminal approaching it without a key. There was a fairly large hall under a staircase in the Relatives' and Visitors' Centre, where families were waiting, with children hanging about, bored, demanding attention. A trolley with tea, coffee and soft drinks was being pushed around, a baby was crying. Barry took us into Dr Khan's office, where a young doctor was seeing off a worried mother whose son was still unconscious after an operation. She left the room slowly, unconvinced by his cheerful assurance, and then I had a chance to inspect the desk.

The drawer was locked, but Bernard had been to see Tiffany to get the key. It was a small brass key for a small brass lock which, again, wouldn't have presented much of a problem to experienced lock pickers on either side of the law.

The drawer slid open and revealed a surprising spectacle, uncharacteristic of the neat and self-contained Dr Khan. The drawer was a mess. If it had been any bigger it might have been called a tip. There were pieces of old circulars, letters, credit-card bills, notes on patients, doctors' requests, tubes of sweets, a half-full bottle of pills, a slightly tattered copy of *Health & Beauty* magazine. I glanced at the letters but there was nothing that could have been in any way incriminating. I shut the drawer and locked it.

'*If* he's not guilty . . .' I started when we returned to Barry's room in the main hospital, but he jumped in before I could finish my sentence.

'*If?*' he said. 'What's "*if*" about it? Surely we all believe Mahmood's innocent, don't we?'

'Do we?' I warned. 'Have you read the letters? I asked Bernard to send you copies.'

'Disgusting!' Barry agreed. 'But I can't believe Mahmood was involved in any of that. They might have sent him the letters, I suppose.'

'What for?'

'What for? To trap him perhaps. To make him join them. What does Mahmood say about the letters?'

'He says he's never seen them before in his life. They came as a complete surprise to him. That's what he says.' Barry said nothing to that, so I went on, 'Do you still believe he's innocent?'

'Of course I do. Don't you?'

'I'm not sure,' I answered him cautiously. 'But I'm prepared to act on that assumption.'

'That's terrible for Mahmood!' Barry was clearly shocked. 'Terrible if his own barrister doesn't believe he's innocent.'

'My beliefs, one way or the other, are completely irrelevant. I shall defend him to the best of my ability, and I don't think he, or you, will have a fault to find with the Rumpole ability. Can we still rely on you as a character witness?'

'Of course you can.' Barry was looking at me doubtfully. 'The question is – can we rely on you?'

'I think I've already answered that question.' I gave a brisk answer to a man who seemed unwilling to trust his friend's fate to Rumpole.

In the weeks that followed I did my best to forget the doubting Barrington and return to the Rumpole confidence, which, I am delighted to say, was soon back and supporting me loyally through a number of minor cases.

One unoccupied afternoon my thoughts turned again to Will Timson – the Timson who hated Dr Khan and wanted to see him behind bars, a result that had been achieved. I looked through the brief and discovered, among the list of items removed from his garage by the police, mainly consisting of television sets, iPods and DVDs, a folder containing 'lists, notes and addresses'. Purely on a whim, a hundred-to-one off-chance, I asked Bonny Bernard to inspect this file and copy anything that seemed important.

Days later he rang me. 'It's the damnedest thing. I can't imagine how you got on to it. In the file there's a paper with our Dr Khan's address and telephone number and his contact number at the hospital. Oh, and there's more still. It's in that Indian language. Shall I get it translated?'

'Yes,' I said, delighted by his news. 'Do you think we're going to find out something helpful at last?'

'I don't know about that,' Bernard said, 'but I do know what judge we've got assigned to us.'

'Who?' I asked, and his answer wiped the smile off my face.

'The new judge. The one they've just appointed. Bullingham.'

The news couldn't have been worse. I wondered if it would help if I thought of him as 'Leonard'.

28

Extract from Hilda Rumpole's Memoirs

'Will Timson hates Dr Khan. Will Timson has in his possession Dr Khan's telephone number and also a document written in Urdu. On being translated, this appears to be a note of some of the facts which appear in the incriminating letters directed to Dr Khan and apparently found in his possession. Is this a chink of light? The beginning of a defence?'

'I do wish you'd stop whingeing on about that wretched Dr Khan's case, Rumpole,' I told him. 'It's not good for your health.' I had done lamb chops with mashed potatoes, which is what he usually likes, but he was just picking at it.

'It would mean that Will was in contact with some sort of terrorist or terrorist organization. It's not improbable. He could have done a bit of research among prisoners or ex-prisoners. Speakers of Urdu. It's not impossible, is it? Or what do you think?'

'I think if you're not going to eat up the nice dinner I cooked for you you'll have to go back on the Omni Vite.'

This had its effect. Rumpole started on a chop. But he hardly ever discussed his cases with me unless I brought up the subject first. I could see he was worried about defending the extremely dodgy Dr Khan, and he had every reason to be so. If he would take on absolutely laughable cases, he had only himself to blame.

'You really have no need to worry,' I did say, just to cheer him up. 'You'll have a perfectly fair trial in front of Leonard Bullingham. Why can't you leave it all to him?'

'A fair trial!' Rumple spluttered. He choked on his mashed potato and had to rectify matters by a giant swig of his Very Ordinary claret. 'Expecting a fair trial from the newly crowned Mr Justice Bullingham is like expecting a penguin to dance "The Merry Widow Waltz". The Mad Bull would have no instinct for fair trial if it stood up and shouted in his face.' Then he must have seen my look of disapproval, because he added, 'Although, Hilda, I know he took you to lunch at the Sheridan Club.'

'He did,' I told him. 'And he managed to get through his meal without spitting out mashed potato.' Of course I didn't tell him about my visit to the cinema with Leonard, or the fact that he had made what amounted to a proposal. I don't think Rumpole would have quite understood if I'd told him that. So I just cleared away the dinner and left Rumpole sitting staring into the gas fire, smoking too many of his small cigars. I knew exactly what he was thinking about. 'Please, Rumpole,' I said, 'keep Dr Khan out of here. I have to say, he's not welcome in Froxbury Mansions.'

Dodo came up to London to see the Augustus Johns. She came to stay and of course she was full of the little Frenchman she'd met on her sketching trip to France. 'Lu-Lu, we called him,' she said. 'Of course, his real name was Louis, but we all called him Lu-Lu and I think he rather liked it. You know, Hilda, he had that way of talking to you which makes you feel like a woman.'

Well, I didn't know what else Dodo would feel like when anyone talked to her. A man? A child? Or even some animal? In Dodo's case I saw her for a moment as a large furry dog, with big eyes and a tendency to jump upon the furniture. We were having lunch in Fortnum's and I dismissed that idea from my mind.

'Did he propose marriage to you, Dodo?' was what I asked her.

'Of course not. Frenchmen don't think about marriage, do they? Marriage is the last thing on their minds.'

'I don't know about Frenchmen.' And then I said, quite casually, 'I had a proposal of marriage, but of course he was an Englishman.'

'Good heavens!' Dodo seemed really startled. 'Does Rumpole know about this?'

'No, of course he doesn't know. And I shan't tell him unless he gets really irritating.'

'Well!' I could see that Dodo was fascinated by my news. 'Who is this Englishman?'

'I'm not at liberty to tell you that.'

'Why ever not?' Dodo looked slightly hurt.

'He's a well-known public figure, Dodo. That's why.'

'You mean he's someone on television?'

'No, Dodo. He's not on television. He's someone of particular importance in the legal profession. And that's all I'm going to tell you.'

'Oh, well,' Dodo looked pleased that it wasn't a television star, 'if it's someone high up in the legal profession I've probably never heard of him.'

'He's just received an important appointment. And do you know what he wants?'

'Of course I don't, and are you quite sure that you do, Hilda?' was what Dodo said.

'He wants me to divorce Rumpole and, well, he wants me to marry him. He says he's lonely.'

'That's what those sorts of men say, they always say they're lonely. But of course, he's a lawyer, isn't he?'

'I told you that.'

'Well, you can't trust what lawyers say. Look at Rumpole. He'll get up in court and say absolutely *anything*. Now, it's quite different with people in the *arts*. Great artists are almost always sincere.'

'You're not going to tell me that your little Frenchman is a great artist, are you?'

'He's not been discovered yet. But he did a study of a haystack when we were in the Dordogne, and I'm here to tell you, Hilda, it was quite as good as Monet.'

'Is he as good as Augustus John?'

'Oh, much better than Augustus John.'

For the rest of the lunch I didn't have much to say to Dodo. She was just like that at school, she always had a great deal to tell you and was never interested in anyone else's news. I shall be quite glad when she goes back to Lamorna Cove.

29

'Will Timson says he never looked inside the file. Never wrote Khan's number in there. Knows nothing about notes in Urdu. In fact, he denies everything.'

'That's what the Timson family were taught as soon as they learned to speak. Deny everything.' This was my reaction to Bonny Bernard's latest instructions as we walked together across the yard in Brixton Prison on our way to the interview room and a routine visit to Dr Khan. There were two prisoners weeding a flower bed, a warden leading a large dog, a patch of open sky in early autumn. Brixton is one of the time-honoured, or dishonoured, institutions in our country, which confines more people to prison than any other in Europe. This pattern of offending and reoffending continues because nobody seems able to think of anything better to do with the Timsons and their like. It's ridiculous, but I now get an uneasy feeling whenever I visit a prison that somewhere someone is preparing a serious charge against me and that I might, one day, be led off down a long corridor by a man with a clinking bundle of keys to be locked up and take my dinner seated on the lavatory.

Nothing like that happened, of course, and we were soon paying a courtesy visit to our client, sitting in a room where a lonely cactus wilted and we could see the back of a warden's head through the glass panel in the door.

Dr Khan shook his head when Bonny Bernard offered him a cigarette, an automatic gesture my instructing solicitor always indulges in when meeting prisoners.

'No, thank you, Mr Bernard. My troubles have not led me to take up smoking. Nor to taking drugs, although they are freely available in here.' This was followed by a short and completely mirthless laugh.

'Will Timson hates you very much, doesn't he?' I asked the question.

'He is exceedingly jealous. I can understand that, considering the beauty of my wife.'

'All the same, you shouldn't have telephoned him to warn him off.'

'Clearly not. They put me in prison for it.'

'Will Timson was found in possession of papers with your address and telephone number and notes in Urdu which clearly contemplate acts of terrorism.'

'It sounds familiar.'

'Something like the letter they say you received.'

'They say that. I never received them.'

'Do you think Will Timson hates you so much he was trying to frame you?'

'I don't know about that.' Dr Khan considered the idea and seemed to like it. 'He would have needed help, from someone who could write letters in Urdu, I suppose. Could he have got such help?'

'Possibly. I've always thought of Will as one of the cleverer Timsons.' Then I remembered, perhaps a little late, that Will Timson was my client and I was bound to put the case for the defence. 'He says the documents in question were part of the booty a friend of his took from a corner shop off the Edgware Road.'

'Corner shop?' Dr Khan repeated my words with something like affection.

'Well, I don't know if this one is actually on a corner. And it doesn't sell interesting groceries any more – it's all computers and television sets and iPods. It's in Heckling Street so far as I remember.'

'Heckling Street.' He was smiling as though I had mentioned some beautiful place where he had played as a child. 'Numbers 33 to 35.'

'You know it?'

'Of course. It was one of my father's favourite shops. The one he was most proud of.'

'You don't still own it?'

'No, of course not. I told you, my father lost all his shops.'

Well, that was a relief. At least I didn't have to contend with one client stealing from another. But Dr Khan seemed determined to tell me the story of his father's corner shop and I composed myself to listen.

'It was all bad luck really. The shops were going so well and suddenly trouble started. Then there was nothing but trouble.'

'What sort of trouble?'

'Silly things at first. Small things. Things went missing. Then the stealing got more serious. There was a fire in one shop. Then the ordering went wrong, stuff never got delivered. And then the managers kept leaving. He couldn't keep a manager for more than a week or so before they quarrelled with the rest of the staff. It was beginning to get my dad down, I think, so he sold them all off.'

'All to one buyer?'

'No. To different buyers. I can't remember who they

were, in fact I doubt if he ever told me. He didn't talk about it much. I think he was ashamed of having failed in his business. Anyway, he was left with nothing but his savings and the beautiful house we live in. At the very end I was keeping him.'

'He didn't think of selling the house?'

'No. Dad was so proud of the house he would never have sold it. And I hope never to sell it either,' then he added with a smile, 'if you can keep me out of prison, Mr Rumpole.'

I wasn't in a position to guarantee him anything so I asked, 'Did the shops do better after he sold them?'

'I suppose so. I don't really know. His Heckling Street shop seems to have done well enough to be worth stealing from, doesn't it?'

'It's a sad story. About your father.'

'Not altogether sad. He loved Tiffany. He had good friends like Mr Jubal.'

'Mr Jubal? Who was he?'

'Benazir's father. And my dad's friend. That's how we know Benazir.'

'Mrs Barry Whiteside?'

'Yes. You know, it was strange. My father told me this odd thing. The Jubals and the Khans had been deadly enemies in Pakistan. The two families had hated each other for years. It was some dispute over a piece of land, something like that. But when they met in England, my father and Benazir's father forgot all about the family feud and they became firm friends. Perhaps it had something to do with your British climate.' Dr Khan seemed to have made a little joke; in the unlikely surroundings of Brixton Prison he giggled.

'My father always said, when he was down on his luck and had lost all his shops, "I am still a lucky man, I've got you and a good friend. And of course I've got the house."'

'The house was very important to him?'

'Whatever bad luck he had, he said, "I've kept this house, and you'll keep it for me, won't you, Mahmood?" I promised I would on the day he died.'

He was silent for a while, as though to impress upon us the solemnity of his oath, and then he said, 'You'll win this case for me, won't you, Mr Rumpole? Tiffany has so much confidence in you.'

'I'll do my best,' was all I could tell him. And I wished I had as much confidence in myself.

30

'We must be prepared for all eventualities,' I told Bonny Bernard when he came for a conference in my chambers, 'even the unlikely possibility that Will Timson is telling us the truth.'

'What do you mean exactly?'

'Just that even if these scraps of paper have nothing to do with him, we're left with the following facts. A shop in Heckling Street, at one time the property of our client's father, contained a paper with Dr Khan's name and address on it and a document written in Urdu with notes apparently connected with terrorist activity.'

'So what do you suggest?'

'I suggest we make use of the services of Fig Newton. He could visit Heckling Street and tell us what he can find out about that particular corner shop and its proprietor.'

'You really think that's going to help us?'

'God only knows. But we've got to try everything.'

Ferdinand Ian Gilmour Newton, of the aged mackintosh and perpetual cold caught from keeping close observation on bedroom windows during long and rainy nights, was, I knew, the man to prise out any nuggets of information that might be found in the corner shop. I could think of no further lines of investigation, and when Bonny Bernard left me I lit a small cigar and contemplated the situation.

I, who had complained of the lack of work, was now faced with two cases which gave every appearance of inevitable losers. Will Timson had been found with stolen property and Dr Khan with incriminating letters in his possession. Will had criminal form and Dr Khan would be regarded with the hatred and contempt rightly felt for anyone remotely connected with terrorism. No jury would feel any hesitation in convicting either of them. Furthermore, in Khan's case we had drawn the short straw of the Mad Bull, newly appointed to the scarlet and ermine on the bench and no doubt convinced that it was his public duty to pot the doctor, a task which would require no particular effort or intellectual ability.

It was the Mad Bull, I remembered, who had given lunch to She Who Must Be Obeyed in the hallowed precincts of the Sheridan Club. What was that all about? Had he done it simply to irritate Rumpole? If so, it seemed a curiously circuitous and costly way of doing it. He had every opportunity of doing that at public expense when we were in court together. Could it be, could it possibly be, that the recently appointed Mr Justice Bullingham had taken something of a shine to Hilda? And hadn't she, after their lunch together, spoken unreasonably well of him? I found this line of thought disturbing, even life-threatening, like the small jolt at the start of an earthquake. Could it be . . . could it possibly be? I decided to dismiss this train of thought from my mind and cross the road to the comfort of Pommeroy's Wine Bar.

I was foiled in this pursuit by a rap at the door and the immediate entrance of another, far more personable judge, Mrs Justice Phillida Erskine-Brown, once my pupil and the Portia of our chambers, fresh off the bench and apparently on her way home.

'I thought I'd just pop in and say hello, Rumpole,' she said. 'Keeping busy, are you?'

'Up to my eyes. Two extremely heavy cases.'

'I'm glad to hear it. And how are things in chambers?'

'How are things? Sam Ballard is as pompous as ever and is insisting on enquiring into any failure to contribute to the coffee-making. Henry has fallen in love with a secretary from Paper Buildings and forgets to collect fees earned long ago. Miss Gribble thinks I'm ruining my image by defending in a terrorist case. And the upstairs loo is out of order again.'

'So it's all much as usual?'

'Yes. Much as usual.'

'I want to have a word with you about that terrorist case you're doing.'

'Oh, do you?'

'I know you had a word with Fred about it at our party.'

'Yes, I did. Mr Sugden was very cooperative.'

'Fred is. He believes passionately in British justice and our legal system.'

'He does now. He wasn't so keen on a fair trial for my client before your party.'

'He's an important politician, Rumpole. He has to deal with Special Branch and the Foreign Office and public opinion, which wants to see people like Dr Khan locked up without question. But he saw your point and there's going to be a trial. I think that was very brave of him.'

'Very brave.' I was going to tell my former pupil the

reason for Sugden's sudden change of heart, but decided not to.

'You must have been very persuasive.'

'I can be persuasive.'

'I know you can, Rumpole. And I'm sure you'll agree that Fred has behaved very well in this situation.'

I began to have an idea of what was coming, so I looked at her without answering for a while and then I said, 'Claude says you've taken rather a shine to him.'

Phillida wasn't fazed by this remark. She simply said, 'I do find his personality attractive.'

'What does Claude think about that?'

'Oh, Claude has other interests, doesn't he?'

'Not at the moment. He seems deeply in love with his strange job at SIAC.'

'He's doing well there. Fred says they're very pleased with him.'

'Well, that's nice for everyone, isn't it?'

She ignored this and said, 'Come along, Rumpole. Your doctor hasn't got a hope in hell, has he?'

'I don't know about hell. However, we have hope until the jury come back and say he's guilty.'

'Aren't those letters absolutely conclusive of his guilt?'

'Of someone's guilt perhaps.'

'I think that what Fred feels is that he's allowed the matter to go before the court.'

'Very decent of him . . .'

'Yes. And of course Special Branch are dead set on a conviction. If you're planning any lawyer's tricks you think might get him off . . .'

'What sort of tricks is he suggesting? It might be helpful to know.'

'Isn't this a case, Rumpole,' she chose to look straight into my eyes, 'when a guilty plea is probably in the best interests of the client?'

'He tells me he's innocent.'

'But you don't really believe that, do you?'

'I have to put his case.'

'It's in no one's interest, Rumpole.'

'Your precious Fred wants to see him shut up.'

'It's not just Fred. I've told you what I think too.'

'*Et tu, Portia?*' Soon after that she left.

31

'Mr Molloy, the hatred between the Timsons and the Molloys is legendary, is it not? It exceeds the hatred of the Montagues and the Capulets.'

'Mr Rumpole,' a friendly voice called gently from the bench. It was old Denny Densher, once and quite briefly of our chambers, who was probably the most tolerable of the Old Bailey judges. 'Your literary allusions may be lost on the jury. Try Arsenal and Spurs.'

'I'm much obliged.' I really was. 'Does your family hate the Timsons as much as the two football teams?'

'We found the Timsons a load of creeps as a general rule, yes.'

'What do you mean by creeps? That they had a tendency to grass, become police informers, anything like that?'

'That among other things, yes.'

'What other things?'

'Well, you just wouldn't trust them.'

'And yet you became friends with Will Timson.'

'We met at a party and had a few drinks. He was all right.'

'So much all right that you suggested he join you in a job at the shop in Heckling Street.'

'I've already admitted that.'

'A shop on the Edgware Road was far out of the

Timson area of operation, wasn't it? Was the whole thing your idea?'

'Will Timson agreed to it. Only too pleased, he was.'

'I suggest he didn't agree. He looked at the shop with you by daylight and said it wasn't safe, it was too near the main road. He had all sorts of objections.'

'He was only too pleased to do the job with me. That's what I told the inspector.'

James Molloy was short with broad shoulders that seemed unusually high so that his face seemed to sink between them. His thick black eyebrows were fixed in a perpetual frown. He spoke in a husky voice, a sort of outraged whisper.

'You got a lot of advantages from what you told the inspector, didn't you?'

'I don't know what you mean.'

'Oh yes, you do. Eighteen months' sentence already passed on you. Less than half of the normal tariff.'

'I told him the truth. That's all.'

'Let's see if you did. Did you take your van to the shop that night?'

'Will didn't have a van.'

'So it was yours. You'd had a look at the burglar alarm on a previous visit. Was it you who disconnected it on the night?'

'Will didn't know much about burglar alarms.'

'So you did it?'

'I had to.'

'And after you'd loaded your van, you drove it back to your house?'

'Yes.'

'And not to Will's?'

'No.'

'In fact you only took it to Will's three days later. Why did you take it to him?'

'Because he's got more room round his garage and that.'

'Or was it so that he would be arrested if anything went wrong?'

'I expected him to dispose of it. To get the best price he could.'

'He didn't dispose of it, did he? The goods you stole were still in his garage when the police arrested him.'

'Not my fault he was so slow on the job.'

It was an unusual morning in court. The judge was listening and not interrupting, the jury were listening carefully and I had the best of my cross-examination to come.

'You were caught because the CCTV camera got a picture of you driving your van away. It was a picture that was pretty clear to the police.'

'I reckoned without that camera.'

'Exactly. But there was no picture on the cameras showing that Will was in the van with you.'

'He was in the back of the van. The camera wouldn't see him.'

'Is that what you're telling this jury?'

'That's what I'm telling them, yes.'

I allowed the jury a moment's silence before I delivered the punchline.

'Mr Molloy, you just told me that members of the Timson family grass and aren't to be trusted.'

'That's right. That's what they do. Yes.'

'And you have proved yourself the biggest grass in this case.'

'Just in this case.'

'And, as a grass, I don't suppose you really expect this jury to trust you.'

I sat down then, and a flurry of re-examination from the prosecution didn't do much to restore anyone's confidence in James Molloy. After that I didn't put Will Timson, whom I had persuaded to plead guilty to the charge of receiving stolen property, in the witness box.

I relied on a speech to the jury to persuade them that Mr James Molloy was not a reliable witness, and they didn't need a great deal of persuading. Will Timson was acquitted on the robbery charges.

So far as the receiving went, Denny Densher successfully found that he wasn't a professional fence, that there were no previous convictions for receiving and he was disposed to pass a sentence of eighteen months suspended, in view of the fact that all the property had been recovered and Will had spent a considerable time in custody.

'Suspended sentence!' Outside the court Will seemed truly amazed. 'So I walk free?'

'Unless you do another crime,' I reminded him. 'Then they can make you serve the eighteen months.'

'I don't recollect any of the family getting a suspended before.'

'Neither do I.'

'I've got to thank you, Mr Rumpole. Anything I can do for you?'

I looked at him. Did I trust him? Of course I didn't. All the same I tried. 'You can tell me all you know about the letters found in Dr Khan's desk.'

'Nothing. I don't know anything about that. All I know about that man is that he's a bloody terrorist.

They're not going to give *him* a suspended sentence, are they?'

'No,' I assured the man who hated the doctor. 'No one's going to get him anything like that.'

I began these memoirs with a Timson case lost and am drawing towards the conclusion with a Timson case which was, at least, more successful. Will had gone off wearing his suspended sentence as though it were some kind of award, distancing him from the rest of the family. But I couldn't forget his hatred of Dr Khan, or the fact that he had been indirectly responsible for the enigmatic doctor's move from the sunny side of Kilburn to Brixton Prison. Was there any way, any conceivable way, that he could have been connected with the packet of Urdu letters found in Dr Khan's desk?

The successful result in Will's case had put a certain amount of spring in the Rumpole step and the autumn sun seemed to shine more brightly. But now we were moving into darker skies and no doubt far less happy months. Terrorism and fear of terrorists had increased in the world. Every news bulletin brought details of new explosions, assassinations, religious hatred and wanton death. If there was any doubt in Dr Khan's case, I didn't expect he'd get the benefit of it.

But my investigations were not complete. Fig Newton was still beavering away and at last he was ready with his report. He had made further enquiries into the affairs of Baltistan-British Services Ltd. The company had been founded some fifteen years ago to take possession of a number of shops and 'retail premises', including the shop in Heckling Street. Fig had written down the names of the original founder and chairman of the company (now deceased) and the names of the present chairman and the directors. I read all this with considerable interest.

After I had read his report I met Fig with Bonny Bernard in Pommeroy's to ask for further details. He sat nursing his ginger beer ('Keep off the alcohol,' he said, 'if you want to be an efficient private detective') and sniffing with his perpetual cold.

He had been to the Heckling Street shop, where he met the Pakistani manager, Ali Raza. When he asked Mr Raza about the notes in Urdu which had been stolen from his shop, Fig Newton said that he was a detective, which was true, and that he was just checking up on a few facts. Mr Raza, apparently anxious to cooperate with the police, gave Fig a great deal of information of extraordinary interest.

It was when Fig had finished his account of the interview in the Heckling Street shop that I felt that a shaft of light had pierced the gloom surrounding Dr Khan's case. I thanked heaven for Mr Raza and his innocence in assuming that Fig was a member of Special Branch. I told Bonny Bernard to issue a witness summons and, for the first time, I was looking forward to *R.* v. *Khan* with something like eager anticipation.

32

Extract from Hilda Rumpole's Memoirs

I don't know why, but we have now entered a period when Rumpole is cock-a-hoop, which is something I find rather irritating. So far as I can see he's got absolutely nothing to be cock-a-hoop about. It's November, very windy and dark most of the time. There is a simply enormous bill for the electricity which Rumpole seems reluctant to pay; he has a tendency to keep bills to mature as though they were old bottles of wine. The bridge club has got dull since Leonard has been on the High Court bench, or away on circuit, and I still haven't quite forgiven Dodo for what she said about Leonard and her fat little (I'm sure he must be fat) sketching teacher, who is apparently more important than a High Court judge because he's a 'great artist'. Like Monet indeed! Well, I bet I there won't be queues waiting outside the Tate to see Dodo's sketching teacher's haystacks in fifty years' time. Of course I shall make things up with Dodo in the future, but in the meantime I'm going to let her stay where she is, which is Lamorna Cove.

I also can't understand why Rumpole should feel cock-a-hoop about the Khan case, which is due to come on at the end of the month. Everyone from the Lord Chancellor to Mrs O'Mally, who comes to clean three times a week, must be absolutely certain he's guilty and we're only going through the motions of a trial to show the world how fair British justice is, even to terrorists.

All the same, Rumpole stays cock-a-hoop. I heard him sing as he cleaned his teeth in the bathroom one morning what must now be one of the oldest songs in living memory.

> 'He'd fly through the air with the greatest of ease,
> That daring young man on the flying trapeze.'

When he emerged I said, 'Rumpole, what on earth's the matter with you? Have you fallen in love with somebody?' I have had that trouble in the past, particularly concerning a girl he met in the air force called Bobby Dougherty, married to an ex-policeman, Sam 'Three Fingers' Dougherty, whom Rumpole took every opportunity of visiting in a dreadful pub they kept at some ghastly seaside resort.

'Yes,' he said. 'I love someone.' He's not usually so frank when I ask him that sort of question.

'Not that awful RAF woman again?'

'Nothing like it. This is a man with a perpetual cold and who goes by the name of Ferdinand Ian Gilmour Newton. A private detective.'

'Rumpole, I wish you'd stop talking nonsense.'

'It's not nonsense, it's a defence. Some sort of a defence at least.' And then he looked anxious. 'If only I knew how to make it work.'

'You mean you're going to fight *R.* v. *Khan*?'

'Of course I am.' He looked quite insulted. 'What did you think I was going to do?'

A fight, I thought, and who was it going to be between? Leonard and Rumpole, whom I suppose you might call the men in my life. I suddenly had an absurdly romantic picture of the Elizabethan ladies who sat holding their fans or eating sweetmeats while a couple of knights crashed swords with each other for their favours. If the Khan trial wasn't going to be as dramatic, it couldn't be duller than sitting in the flat with a frozen vegetable curry and the ten o'clock news.

'Rumpole,' I said, 'it's a long time since I saw you in action.'

To my surprise, he looked a little sheepish. 'I've been tired in the evenings,' he said, 'and the pressure of work . . .'

'I mean, it's a long time since I saw you in action in court. Doing an important case. I used to go to court to see Daddy's important cases. Of course, you don't have as many as he did, but this is one that's bound to get into all the papers. I thought I might come along, just to see how you and Leonard deal with the whole affair. You wouldn't have any objections to that, would you?'

It seemed to take him a while to think about it, but then he said, 'No objection in the world, Hilda, but you do realize I shall be rather busy?'

'Of course you will. And Leonard will be very busy too. It'll just be interesting to watch you both at work.'

33

'So we meet again.'

'Yes indeed, we met at Philippi.'

'Philip what?' Peter Plaistow, QC, MP, dressed in full courtroom fig, looked painfully confused.

'*Julius Caesar*,' I explained. 'The place of the final battle. I take it that Shakespeare is not one of New Labour's favourite authors.'

'Really? Who won?'

'Look it up for yourself.' If I'd answered his question I'd've had to admit it was the government, the establishment in the shape of Mark Antony and Octavius Caesar and Lepidus the moneybags, so I said, 'More to the point, let's see who's going to win this battle. Now we've got a fair trial.'

'I expect to get a bit of help from the learned judge.' Peter Plaistow gave me his most charming smile. 'Dear old Bullingham's the last person to be soft on terrorists.'

'I don't know. I've got a feeling that the Mad Bull has shown a tender side of his nature lately.'

'Don't be ridiculous. There isn't a tender side to Bullingham. By the way, Rumpole, there's a woman waving at you from the public gallery.'

I looked up and who should I see but Hilda, whom I had left after breakfast two hours before, looking down at me from beside the clock in the front row of the circle.

She raised her hand in a sort of salute and I raised mine back. She looked vaguely imperial and I remembered the circus in ancient Rome. I thought of the gladiators' cry of 'We who are about to die salute you.'

'That happens to be my wife,' I told Plaistow. 'So you better watch it. And let me tell you, her father was a notable QC, so she has high standards and isn't afraid of letting her views be known. And also let me tell you, my client isn't a terrorist. He's innocent now and will be until . . .'

'I know,' Plaistow gave me a patronizing smile, 'until the jury comes back with a verdict. You're so predictable, Rumpole.'

'And you believe that everyone's guilty the moment the government says so. Perhaps that's the difference between us.'

Tiffany Khan took her seat behind me, her hand clutching a crumpled handkerchief that had dried her tears. She was doing her best to be brave and looking as beautiful as when she was beside the clock in the public gallery, looking down on me to check my performance. With her was a neatly dressed grey-haired man, perhaps in his sixties, whom she introduced as her dad, Ray Timson, who had been fingered so rarely by the police that I couldn't remember ever having had to defend him.

'We were against the marriage in the first place,' Ray explained, 'but now Tiffany's old man's in such trouble, I thought I'd come along and give her my support. You'll do your best for him, won't you, Mr Rumpole?'

'Oh yes, I'll do my best.' I didn't tell him that my best might not be good enough.

'Where's Barry?' Tiffany looked round, in a sort of panic at the absence of her faithful supporter.

'He's a witness,' I explained. 'A character witness. So they're keeping him outside the court.'

'I thought I saw Will sat there too, Will Timson. What's he here for?'

There was no time for an answer. An enthusiastic usher called out, 'Be upstanding!' and Mr Justice Bullingham, in all his new-found glory, sailed into the court and took possession of the case.

Half an hour later the jury was sworn in and Peter Plaistow was soon winning their hearts with his opening speech. It was a standard jury, five men and seven women, including a studious-looking Chinese woman, an eager young man who might have been a schoolteacher, a powerful middle-aged black mother and no doubt ruler of a Caribbean family, a *Telegraph*-reading businessman in an old school tie who looked resentful, no doubt because he had far more lucrative business somewhere else, a serious young woman, perhaps a journalist, who was already taking notes, a fat man in a checked open-necked shirt who was ready to laugh at Peter Plaistow's feeble attempts at a joke and who would, I was sure, be the life and soul of the jury room, a young couple who seemed pleased to find themselves sitting next to each other, and a formidable woman in her fifties who sighed wearily from time to time as though she had not yet forgiven everyone in court, including the judge or his prisoner, for dragging her into Court Number One at the Old Bailey on a windy November morning.

Plaistow took them through the story. Dr Khan's flight from Pakistan, apparently for some obscure political reason, his success as a doctor and his inheritance of his father's house in Kilburn, and then the police suspicion which caused him to be followed. 'On one occasion,' Plaistow told them, 'Dr Khan visited a house in Highfield Road, Willesden, the house of suspected terrorists, well known to the police, who have subsequently been arrested and confined in Belmarsh Prison.

'And now, members of the jury,' Plaistow was no longer jovial but alarmingly serious, 'we come to the most serious and utterly alarming part of this case, the letters found in Dr Khan's desk, under lock and key at Oakwood Hospital.'

'I wish to make it quite clear to this jury,' I had risen, probably unwisely, to my feet at this point, 'that Dr Khan denies any knowledge whatsoever of these letters.'

'Isn't my learned friend a little *too* eager to give us his denial?' Peter Plaistow talked to the judge as though they were old friends sharing a drink at the Sheridan Club.

'Yes, indeed. Your time will come, Mr Rumpole. There's absolutely no need for you to jump the gun.' The Mad Bull was smiling and, to my surprise, I saw him transfer the smile to the public gallery, where She Who Must Be Obeyed was sitting, as though in judgement.

I sat down to the worst of welcomes, a look of compassion from my instructing solicitor, Bonny Bernard.

Then Plaistow read out a translation of all the letters. In his clear, matter-of-fact tones, they sounded more shocking than ever. By the end the jury were not looking with horror at the apparently unperturbed doctor in the dock, they turned their faces away and refused to look at him at all.

It was afternoon before I got a chance to cross-examine the Special Branch officer in change of the case. Hilda and

I had lunched on sausages and mash in the company of Bonny Bernard in the Old Bailey canteen.

'You've got an uphill task defending that little doctor, haven't you, Rumpole? The letters . . .'

'Don't tell me, Hilda. I don't need reminding.'

'And Leonard's giving you a perfectly fair trial, isn't he?'

'So far. He hasn't seen any danger of acquittal, so he's relaxed. Just wait until he jumps down into the arena.'

'And who's the prosecutor? He's got such a lovely speaking voice, don't you think?'

'His name's Peter Plaistow and he's a close personal friend of the Prime Minister. There really isn't anything lovely about him.'

'*Such* a good-looking young man.'

'Thank you so much for coming down to the Old Bailey, Hilda,' I said as we finished the sausages, and I struck the note ironic. 'You've been such an encouragement.'

'Oh, I've thoroughly enjoyed myself, and I'm looking forward to watching you trying to make bricks without straw.'

So now I was standing up and, facing the superintendent, trying to find a straw or two to make my bricks with.

'Superintendent, will you tell us when these letters first came into the hands of the police?'

'It was about a year ago. I think it was quite near to Christmas.'

'And how did you get hold of them?'

'A police officer found them. In Dr Khan's desk.'

'Did you know that Dr Khan was away on holiday?'

'That was our information, yes.'

'Did you tell the hospital authorities that you wanted to search Dr Khan's desk?'

'No.'

'Why not?'

'Isn't it obvious, Mr Rumpole?' The Bull didn't jump, but climbed delicately into the arena. 'If the superintendent had done that, Dr Khan would have been warned and might have removed the letters. Is that the situation?'

'Quite right, My Lord.'

'So you are only too pleased to accept His Lordship's answer to my question?' I asked the witness.

'I think I was merely pointing out the obvious situation, Mr Rumpole.' Hilda's Leonard was positively purring.

'I only regret,' and I said this as politely as it was possible for an outraged Rumpole to speak, 'that when you give evidence I have no opportunity of cross-examining Your Lordship.'

Leonard didn't rebuke me for this. Instead he turned to the jury and said, in the friendliest possible way, 'Mr Rumpole is inclined to make these sorts of remarks, members of the jury. They are completely out of order and I advise you to ignore them.' Then he turned to me with a condescending sort of smile and said, 'Have you any further questions to put to this officer, Mr Rumpole?'

I glanced up at the public gallery. I thought I detected, on Hilda's face, a smile of pleasure. Then I got back to work.

'So you acted without a search warrant?'

'Yes, we did.'

'Without the permission of the hospital authorities?'

'I've told you that.'

'So you sent in a Special Branch officer?'

'Yes.'

'Alone?'

'With the assistance of Constable Rogerson.'

'To attack the Relatives' and Visitors' Centre by night?'

'It was night-time, yes.'

'To force the lock on the Relatives' and Visitors' Centre door?'

'They said it didn't give much trouble.'

'I've seen it. It could've been dealt with by any experienced burglar. And they forced the lock on the doctor's desk.'

'They said that didn't give much trouble either.'

'So they came like thieves in the night and stole these letters?'

'They took them, yes.'

'Like common burglars?'

'Or like front-line fighters in the war against terror?' Leonard once again descended into the arena.

'Let me ask you something else, Superintendent.' I was anxious to avoid another exchange of polite insults with Leonard. 'We have had translations of the letters sent to us. I want to ask you about the original documents in Urdu. Did you have them tested for fingerprints?'

'We did.'

'And what was the result?'

'There were no fingerprints on them.'

'None at all?'

'No. Nothing.'

I gave the jury the look of surprise and then turned back to the witness.

'The burgling officers were wearing gloves?'

'As they were instructed to do.'

'There were no envelopes with the letters?'

'We found no envelopes. Perhaps they'd been destroyed.'

'Perhaps they had. But the person, whoever it was, who wrote them, or typed them out, left no prints?'

'None at all. Perhaps whoever typed them wore rubber gloves when handling the paper. They didn't want to be identified.'

'That's a very helpful remark and I hope My Lord and the jury will remember it. But there are none of Dr Khan's prints on the letters, are there?'

'I told you,' the Superintendent sighed. 'But perhaps he didn't want to be identified.'

'So he put on rubber gloves to read the letters and then left them in a drawer at the hospital with a lock that could easily be forced and went off on holiday?' I gave the jury the look of incredulity. 'These terribly incriminating letters?'

'That seems to be what he'd done.'

'A pretty amateurish sort of terrorist, wasn't he?'

'You needn't answer the question,' Leonard advised the witness, who took his advice gratefully. 'That sort of point, Mr Rumpole, is more apt to your final speech.'

'And Your Lordship's comments,' I might have said, 'will be more apt when the case is over. We seem to be getting,' I might have used an old line, 'a case of prosecution adjudication.' But I didn't say any of that, I concentrated on the witness.

'After you had obtained the letters you kept Dr Khan under observation?'

'We did.'

'And he was arrested early in the new year?'

'Yes.'

'You had received information about the letters in his desk?'

'We had.'

'Someone knew he had received the letters and where he kept them?'

'Obviously.'

'Perhaps you'd be good enough to tell My Lord and the jury – who that someone was?'

This question brought Peter Plaistow out of his seat, rising to his feet and protesting that if this superintendent was now being asked to reveal his sources the matter should be ruled on by His Lordship in private. Leonard accordingly invited us into his room. As we left the court I saw Hilda look down at me frowning slightly, as though she were about to be cheated of the best part of the drama.

'The police can't be made to reveal their sources in a terrorist case. It would be far too dangerous for the source and no one would ever dare give the police information again.' This was Plaistow's argument when we got to the judge's room.

'That has to be right, doesn't it, Rumpole?' Leonard was easily persuaded.

'In this case it has to be wrong,' I told him. 'My defence depends on the quality of the information and the nature of the source of it.'

'I'm sorry, Rumpole.' Leonard didn't look too distressed. 'I'm afraid the position is perfectly clear. Special Branch can't be asked to reveal their sources. By the way, Rumpole, we're honoured by the presence of your good lady.'

'His good lady?' Prosecution counsel looked confused.

'Mrs Rumpole is in the public gallery. Taking an interest in our proceedings.' Leonard seemed particularly proud of the fact.

'She came here to see a fair trial,' I told the judge. 'I hope to be able to persuade her that this was a fair trial.'

'I'm sure she'll understand the position about sources.' For the first time Leonard looked a little anxious.

'I'll do my best to explain it to her,' I promised him. 'By the way, if I can't ask about sources I'd like to ask the prosecution to admit certain facts.'

'Such as?'

'That a burglary took place in a shop in Heckling Street, London. Among the articles seized was a paper containing Dr Khan's address and telephone number and some notes in Urdu concerning terrorist activities.'

'There won't be any difficulty about that admission, will there, Mr Plaistow?' I felt the judge was anxious to reassure not so much me as She Who Must Be Obeyed.

'I'm sure there'll be no difficulty, Judge.'

Plaistow clearly thought he could afford a minor concession. So we left the judge's room and I returned to the court with, I felt, one hand tied behind my back. I would have to rely on another route to the source of the information, or misinformation, that had landed my client Khan in the dock.

'I think Leonard was being a bit hard on you, Rumpole,' She Who Must said over our lamb chops that evening in the mansion flat. 'I don't see why you shouldn't know who gave the police the information, even if it's not going to help you at all.'

'Thanks very much, Hilda. I know how sensitive Leonard is to public opinion.'

'On the other hand,' she warned me, 'it's no use you trying to be rude to Leonard.'

'That is one of the facts of life,' I assured her, 'which, however reluctantly, I have learned to accept.'

'Officer B, you say you saw Dr Khan enter the house in Highfield Road, Willesden. How long was it before he came out again?'

'Approximately ten minutes,' the Special Branch operator, who hid under the title of 'Officer B', told the court.

'Approximately ten minutes? Hardly enough to launch a decent plot, was it?'

'He might have been taking instructions. It was a house where we have arrested a known terrorist.'

'And did this known terrorist know anything about Dr Khan?'

'No, but we had other information.'

'Oh yes? From whom exactly?'

'He can't reveal his sources.' Plaistow rose, with exaggerated weariness, to his feet, the judge was in agreement and that was the end of the prosecution case.

I had spoken to Barry Whiteside and he was anxious to get away as soon as possible as he had an important meeting at the hospital. I wanted him as a character witness, I told the judge, so might I take the unusual course of calling him before my client and at the start of the defence case?

I thought I saw Leonard glance up at the public gallery, where She Who Must Be Obeyed had resumed her usual seat beside the clock, almost as though he were seeking instructions. Then he told me that I might call my character witness first if Mr Plaistow had no objection. Plaistow agreed and Barrington Whiteside entered the witness box.

34

'Mr Whiteside,' I started after Barry had been sworn in and recited his credentials, 'as a hospital administrator you have worked with Dr Khan for I think it's fifteen years?'

'Sixteen and a half.'

'And you also knew him as a friend?'

'I am acquainted with him and his wife, yes.'

'An acquaintance? You saw a good deal of each other, you and your wife, Benazir, and him and his wife, Tiffany?'

'We saw a little less of each other lately.'

I looked round the court. On the benches behind me Tiffany was puzzled, shaking her head. Benazir, in her bright sari, gave me a smile. I turned back to the witness box.

'Why was that?'

'Dr Khan seemed changed. He was silent. I thought he was troubled. It was as though he had something on his mind. He didn't seem to want a social life.'

'Really? Mr Whiteside, you know the charges that have been made against your friend Dr Khan?'

'Indeed, I think the whole country does.'

'You're probably right. He is accused of taking part in and encouraging terrorist activities. It's also alleged that he knew of terrorist plans and failed to inform the police. With your knowledge of his character, what is your view of the possibility of any of the charges being true?'

There was a long pause. Barry sipped water from the glass in front of him. Then he started quietly. 'I've said he seemed very remote, withdrawn. I'd say he was worried . . .'

'Speak up, Mr Whiteside.'

'I did feel that he might be engaged in something illegal.' Barry turned up the volume. 'I know he'd been involved in politics of some sort in Pakistan. Looking back on it, I suppose I'd have to admit the charge might be true. Of course I have no evidence . . .'

'No, you haven't have you, Mr Whiteside?' I could not contain my excitement. The witness had walked straight into the trap I had set for him. Now I got the usher to hand him a piece of paper.

'Is that proof of evidence you signed for my solicitor before the hearing of Dr Khan's case before the Special Immigration Appeals Commission?'

'I think so.'

'Just read out what you said about Dr Khan's character then.' And, as Barry appeared reluctant, I had to encourage him. 'Just read it out, please. So we can all hear you.'

'"In my opinion, and I know him extremely well, Dr Khan is incapable of any illegal act and in particular any act of terrorism."'

At which I surprised Barry, and possibly the jury, by asking Mr Justice Leonard Bullingham to rule that I could treat the witness as hostile, the law being that you can't call a witness and cross-examine him unless he has been found to be hostile.

'The witness mustn't just be hostile to Mr Rumpole's client.' Peter Plaistow was on his feet and complaining.

'He must be proved to be hostile to the truth.' Having had his say Plaistow subsided.

'The completely contradictory statements clearly prove this witness is hostile. I have to say that if Your Lordship were to refuse my submission I would have to proceed at once to the Court of Appeal. In the interests of a fair trial for Dr Khan, I feel sure that both the Appeal judges and public opinion would be on my side.' That was the gist of my submission to Leonard.

His Lordship took time for thought. No doubt a newly appointed judge wouldn't wish to be rubbished by the Court of Appeal in one of his first cases; but it might have been public opinion that weighed more with him. To check this he glanced up to the gallery. I'm not sure what the slight frown that She Who Must donated to him was meant to say but, happily, he interpreted it in my favour.

'I find that this witness has been hostile to the truth. You may cross-examine him, Mr Rumpole.'

It was a relief. If this particular ploy hadn't worked I'd have had to think of some other way of bringing the facts of Dr Khan's case before the court.

'Mr Whiteside, you know that when Dr Khan's father came here from Pakistan he acquired about ten corner shops in London.'

'He told me that, yes.'

'And he also acquired a very desirable residence on the better side of Kilburn. I think you admire that house, don't you?'

'Yes, we do. I know my wife and I feel it's a perfect family house.'

'For you?'

'Possibly for us. But of course it belongs to Dr Khan.'

'Who inherited it from his father?'

'Yes.'

'And you would have hoped it would be yours?'

'If Dr Khan didn't own it, yes. I suppose it's the sort of place we'd've liked. But of course it wasn't ours.'

'And Dr Khan and his wife, Tiffany, were your friends?'

'Yes.'

'Good friends?'

'Perfectly good friends.'

'Let's see about that. You know that Dr Khan's father's shops began to fail. There were fires, thefts, all sorts of misfortunes. So in the end he had to sell the shops.'

'I heard something about that.'

'I should rather think you did. The shops eventually became the property of a company called Baltistan-British Services Ltd. And the chairman of the Baltistan was . . . I'm sure you can tell us here, Mr Whiteside? The chairman was Mr Ahmed Jubal. And who was he?'

'My late father-in-law.' The words had to be dragged out of the witness.

'Quite right. And since his death, a director of Baltistan and a major shareholder is none other than your wife, Benazir.'

'Where's all this leading?' Plaistow, QC, MP, rose to his feet a little later than expected. 'I simply wonder where all this talk of companies and corner shops is leading.'

'Then wonder on,' I told the prosecutor, 'till truth make all things plain.'

'Mr Rumpole,' Leonard felt called upon to intervene, 'that's no answer to Mr Plaistow's question.'

'Perhaps not, My Lord. It's a small drop of Shakespeare

– *A Midsummer Night's Dream* – which I thought the court might enjoy. If Your Lordship will allow me to ask the next few questions, I can show exactly where this is leading.'

Once again His Lordship glanced up at the public gallery. Whether he got a clear message of public opinion or not I don't know, but his decision was, 'Very well, Mr Rumpole, but keep it short. We haven't got all the time in the world, you know.'

'I promise Your Lordship I won't take up all the time in the world. Mr Whiteside, one of the shops your wife's company runs is at numbers 33 to 35 Heckling Street, isn't it?'

'It might be.'

'And you know that shop in Heckling Street was burgled, don't you?'

'You should know that, Mr Rumpole.' Here Barrington Whiteside scored his first and only point. 'Didn't you defend one of the burglars?'

There was laughter from the QC, MP, in which the jury joined. As I turned to look at him, I caught Benazir Whiteside in her bright sari staring at me with a look of complete hatred.

'He's rather got you there, hasn't he, Mr Rumpole?' Leonard was pleased as punch, his face wreathed in smiles.

'I was in the case, My Lord. That's why I happen to know so much about it. May I remind the jury of an admission made by the prosecution in their case?'

'Oh very well. If you're coming to the point.'

'This *is* the point. Members of the jury, the prosecution admits that documents stolen from the office of the shop in Heckling Street included a paper with Dr Khan's name on it and notes in the Urdu language referring to various acts of terrorism and suggestions of terrorist activities.'

When they heard that, the jury, who had stopped laughing, became quiet and attentive.

'I don't know anything about that.'

'Don't you? It was your wife's shop.'

'Exactly.'

'And she was a good friend to Dr Khan. Just as her father was a good friend to his father?'

'Of course she was.'

'Was her father such a good friend? Didn't he sabotage the shop and secretly take over the business?'

'I don't know anything about that.'

'And wasn't there something else? A long-term feud between the two families in Pakistan? A hatred of the Khans behind all that pretence of friendship?'

I glanced up at the public gallery. Hilda was leaning forward, apparently listening eagerly to my questions and Barry's answers. I had never received so much attention from her. Then Leonard chipped in with, 'Mr Rumpole, just where is all this leading to?'

'Directly to the question of my client's guilt or innocence. If Your Lordship will just be patient.'

'In my submission, Your Lordship has shown exemplary patience.' Peter Plaistow was on his feet. 'But isn't it now time Mr Rumpole put his case, whatever that may turn out to be?'

'It's in the public interest that I establish the facts leading up to an inevitable conclusion, My Lord,' I told Leonard. 'These are all matters which the public has a right to know.'

I saw Leonard glance up to the public gallery once again and then he said, 'Very well, Mr Rumpole, but the court relies on you to keep it as short as possible.'

'I will be brief. Mr Whiteside, your wife was determined to carry on the family business. Her father had scooped up all the shops, but there was still one great asset the Khan family had left. You wanted it desperately, didn't you?'

'Wanted what exactly?' Barry looked at his wife and attempted a tolerant smile. 'I'm not at all sure what you're talking about.'

'A desirable residence. A fine house on the best side of Kilburn. Ruin Dr Khan and he'd have to sell it to you and your wife at a knock-down price. The Jubal family would have got it all.'

'How do you think we planned to get the house?' Now Barry was asking me a question. I didn't object. I answered him.

'By forging letters about terrorism and leaving them in his desk when he was away on holiday.'

'Mr Rumpole,' Leonard appeared anxious to know, 'are you suggesting that this gentleman and his wife rang up the police and gave them misinformation about your client?'

'Not directly, My Lord. The police informant was Mr Ali Raza, manager of the Heckling Street shop. That's why Dr Khan's name and notes about alleged terrorist activities were found there. He was the so-called source. And if Special Branch want to deny this no doubt my learned friend will have an opportunity of recalling the superintendent.'

Here Plaistow rose, still in a fighting mood, and

promised to take instructions. I turned my attention to Barrington Whiteside again.

'Things were all right for you when my client was in Belmarsh, weren't they? You could pretend to be on his side and hope he'd be stuck there for ever. But then he was given house arrest and planted back in the property you wanted. Was that a bit of a blow to you?'

Barry's smile had faded. He looked sullen and angry, all charm gone.

'I still don't know what you're talking about.'

It was then that I had an idea which considerably shortened the proceedings. Bonny Bernard had served a witness summons on Mr Ali Raza. I asked that he might be brought into court to be identified by Barrington Whiteside.

'You know Mr Ali Raza,' I told Barry, 'who rang Special Branch with the lies you and your wife told. Who sent the text message which asked Dr Khan to visit a terrorist house. And who finally told them to search Dr Khan's desk, where you had hidden the forged letters. Is that Mr Raza?'

Having been called from outside the court, an inoffensive-looking Pakistani of middle age, neatly dressed with spectacles and a greying beard, moved out into the space in front of the witness box.

'You do know Mr Raza, don't you?'

I got no answer to the question. That was the point at which Barrington Whiteside's nerve snapped. His look of fury was now directed at the slim figure in the bright sari who sat on one of the benches behind me.

'It was her idea!' He spat out the words as though afraid of choking on them. 'All hers. She wanted it done. She wanted the house. She wrote the letters. Do you think I could have written them? She got Raza to contact the police. It's all hers, every bit of it, all this stupid business. She wanted it to happen and I'm not paying for it!'

At this he sat on the seat in the witness box and seemed to sob. There was an embarrassed silence in court, so that you could hear the clock by Hilda's seat ticking. And then the silence was broken by Peter Plaistow, who moved to ask for a short adjournment so that the prosecution could consider its position. *R.* v. *Khan* was, in fact, over and the Queen had almost finished her business with the long-suffering doctor.

35

There were formalities to be gone through. The Attorney General had to give Peter Plaistow permission to drop the prosecution. Barry, his wife, Benazir, and Mr Raza from the shop were being interviewed in various parts of the court by various Special Branch officers. The jury had been sent to their room and the judge had left court, and Hilda, I noticed, had vanished from the public gallery.

Tiffany's eyes were full of tears, but this time tears of joy as she stood by the dock looking up at her smiling husband. At last the judge and the jury returned. Peter Plaistow stood up to say that the prosecution would not be proceeding with this case and the jury, in the person of the *Daily Telegraph* reader, who had emerged as the foreman, pronounced a verdict of not guilty.

As they were led away for further interviews, Barry ignored Dr Khan, but Benazir paused to give one of her by now well-known looks of hatred at the prisoner who was being released from the dock, a look which my client returned with a nervous smile. When I said goodbye to him, he said, 'I can't understand it. They were my best friends here in England. I shall miss their company.' And he thanked me, saying he was sorry to have given me so much trouble. As we shook hands, I thought that Dr Khan carried the art of being British to almost ridiculous lengths.

*

'It was a bit of luck, wasn't it, Rumpole? Barrington turning hostile so you could cross-examine him.'

'It's all luck, Hilda. The administration of justice. Life itself. All luck.'

We were having our evening chops in Froxbury Mansions and also sharing a bottle of Pommeroy's Very Ordinary. I was in an expansive, even a philosophic mood and She Who Must seemed unusually interested in my work.

'What would you have done if he hadn't turned hostile and you wouldn't have been able to cross-examine him?' Hilda was also showing an unusual knowledge of the law.

'I'd've found some other way of telling the story.'

'You'd've called that shifty-looking shopkeeper as a witness?'

'I would've had to. I knew what he knew, but I wasn't too sure what he was going to say.'

'You think you're very clever, Rumpole, don't you?' Hilda said after a long pause.

'I think I have a certain talent about the Courts of Law, yes.'

Hilda took a slug of Pommeroy's and told me, 'While you were all waiting about, I was called in to have a cup of tea with the judge.'

'With Leonard?'

'Yes.'

'Did he talk about my talent?'

'Not at all. He talked about another Old Bailey judge. Judge Densher.'

'Denny Densher. A fairly decent type of tribunal.'

'Well, apparently he and Mr Densher take dancing lessons with the same teacher.'

'You surprise me.'

'Well, it seems they do. And Leonard said that if we ever, well, got together, we should take dancing lessons too.'

'He said you might get together?'

'I've never told you that, have I?'

'No, Hilda, you haven't. So did he tell you what was going to happen to me?'

'Well, we were talking about the possibility of a divorce.'

I had an extraordinary feeling that my world was falling apart and I was about to face a strange and unknown future. I saw myself alone in Froxbury Mansions and I was uncomfortably afraid of the prospect.

'We're not getting a divorce, are we?'

'No, Rumpole. We're not.' Hilda's answer came as an unexpected relief. 'We're not going to be divorced. And I'm not going to dancing lessons. I have absolutely no desire to learn the rumba.'

'I'm sure you haven't.'

I refilled Hilda's glass. We drank a while in silence. Then I said, 'Perhaps we should go out more. Perhaps your life's too dull in Froxbury Mansions.'

'Oh, I've got no time to go out,' Hilda told me. 'I shall be far too busy preparing my memoirs for publication.'

'Hilda!' I was astonished. 'You haven't been writing your memoirs?'

'Well, of course I have. You've been writing yours for years, haven't you? Isn't it about time I told my side of the story?'

'Yes.' I wasn't about to argue. 'Yes, of course.' And then I had a sudden insight. 'Is that what you've been doing all this time, locked up in the boxroom?'

'Of course it is.' Hilda gave me a little laugh. 'Didn't you realize? You're not such a great detective as all that, are you, Rumpole?'

Back in chambers at the end of an uneventful day Henry said he had a message. Some friends were anxious to meet me in Pommeroy's. Being headed in that direction anyway, I was surprised to find a group of Timsons, almost as numerous as the committee which decided to dispense with my services. Fred was there, Dennis and Cyril. Percy was still detained and Will was not of the party. The leading Timson on this occasion was clearly Tiffany's father, Ray.

'I can never thank you enough, Mr Rumpole,' he said. 'For what you did for Tiffany. And she can never thank you enough. So I thought it right to bring you back into contact with the family.'

'What Ray has told us,' Dennis sat back in his chair and sounded judicial, 'is that you pulled it off.'

'If you can get a terrorist off you can get anyone off,' was Fred's opinion.

'But he wasn't a terrorist,' I insisted. 'That's why he got off.'

'Whether he was or whether he wasn't,' Dennis remained judicially neutral, 'you got him off. We all have a high opinion of Ray and he speaks highly of your talents – as a brief.'

'I notice that Will isn't here,' I said in the silence that followed.

'Will is still very jealous of your Pakistani friend,' Fred explained. 'But he's extremely grateful for his suspended sentence. Surprised and grateful, Mr Rumpole. We haven't had many of those in the family.'

'If I can express the feelings of the meeting,' Dennis summed up, 'we would like to reappoint you as our official brief, Mr Rumpole. Mr Erskine-Brown has done his best, but we're not satisfied with alternatives that have been found for family members. Would you be prepared to act for us again, Mr Rumpole? If and when the need arises.'

'At any time of the day or night,' I told them. Whereupon Ray bought us all a drink.

So life was back to normal. There would be new closing speeches, further hopefully devastating cross-examinations, more small cigars and further bottles of Château Thames Embankment stretching away into a more or less contented future. There was only one cloud in the sky, at present a cloud no bigger than a man's hand, but who could tell what it might grow to? It was the possible future publication of the memoirs of She Who Must Be Obeyed.